The Invisible Rider

Drawings by Gerard Crewdson

The Invisible Rider

Kirsten McDougall

Victoria University Press

TE WHARE WĀNANGA O TE ŪPOKO O TE IKA A MĀUI

VICTORIA
UNIVERSITY OF WELLINGTON

VICTORIA UNIVERSITY PRESS
Victoria University of Wellington
PO Box 600 Wellington
http://www.victoria.ac.nz/vup

First published 2012

National Library of New Zealand Cataloguing-in-Publication Data

McDougall, Kirsten.
The invisible rider / Kirsten McDougall.
ISBN 978-0-86473-767-0
I. Title.
NZ823.3—dc 23

Published with the assistance of a grant from

ARTS COUNCIL OF NEW ZEALAND *TOI AOTEAROA*

Printed by Printlink, Wellington

For David
and for Marty

Contents

Wildlife   9

Literature   14

The Yellow Scarf   21

Lunar Conversations   40

The Plastic City   44

Laughing Stock   49

Dune Conversations   66

Love   69

The Bookshop   79

Grand Animals   86

Ducks   97

The Insomniacs   102

Secret Life   106

Decay   111

Heart   122

Hunting Reverie   134

Titan Arum   141

Wildlife

It was spring and the valley would shine if the winds weren't battering the place. From his armchair in the attic study, Philip Fetch could look out the window and get a sense of the world. His three apple trees had small budding fruit, but the leaves were rusted and wilting on one side. What he'd imagined as a small orchard with trees that his children could climb and pick apples from was instead a small row of stunted, wind-stung branches. It seemed to Philip that his intentions were often thwarted by external forces. He tried to think practically about a windbreak for his trees, but he was not a person to feel out dimensions for building in his head, and he was distracted by a blackbird tugging at his new lawn. The fat spring bird was pulling tufts of grass out with its beak and leaving the bare earth exposed.

'Hey,' he called out his window.

The bird stopped tugging and looked around briefly but, seeing no immediate threat, went back to work. Hanging his head out the window, Philip clapped his hands and tried to shoo the bird. A gust of wind blew his calls away and the bird whistled out to its friends. Philip watched another three blackbirds settle to work on the same patch of lawn.

The birds worked in a group. They distributed sections of ground seemingly without dispute. Very soon, they had turned the ground over and had started to bob their heads up and down, eating and singing at the same time. The camaraderie they shared! It was a springtime feast, and the workers were celebrating an anticipated return to plenty.

They had also captured the attention of the next-door neighbour's cat, which had come out from its hiding place. The cat was crouched behind a tree. If Philip had liked cats he might have found something to admire in the creature. It had dark grey fur, with white beneath its thick pelt, and a keenly striped tail. Though still a talented hunter, it was actually a bit old and blind, and it took its time to get a feel for the slowest bird in the group.

Philip felt itchy just watching the cat. He also felt a rising tension in his stomach. The house was clear of children. His wife, Marilyn, had taken them to her mother's for the afternoon. Philip had set out a strict timetable of activities for himself. Before him on the desk was the book his good friend James had lent him, *An Introduction to Eastern Moral Philosophy*. Philip intended to work his way through the first chapter at least. Yet here he was getting caught up in a drama he would rather be oblivious to. Surely, though, the cat was doing him a service. The birds were ruining the lawn even before the children had got to it. This was nature, red in tooth and claw. He had no place interfering. But then, the cat and the birds were being forced to play out their true natures in the suburbs. Both, to a certain extent, had a human imprint on them and so it fell to him to provide the necessary care. It's a topsy-turvy world we live in, he thought. He would do what he could to put things right.

Philip picked up the book and put a thick rubber band around it. He hung his head out the window, and estimated a space between the birds and the cat below him. Squinting his right eye, he dropped the book from the second floor of his house. It fell like a brick. The book caught the cat's shoulder and knocked it to the ground. The birds scattered and the cat lay panting on its side.

Philip wanted to slink back into his study chair. The children and Marilyn would arrive home and say, There's a dead cat on our lawn.

It was only a cat. He had been trying to help the stupid birds.

He looked back out the window. 'Stay there!' he said to the cat, and rushed downstairs.

Outside, a small red-faced child was looking over his fence.

'Is this your cat?' said Philip. 'It's been hurt.' He bent over the creature, hoping the child might go away.

The cat was breathing heavily and, though it tried to move, it could not.

'A book fell on Muffin,' said the child. She seemed more curious than concerned.

'A book? How strange,' said Philip. He gave a surprised

look. 'Ah yes, this book. I've been holding a window open with it. It must have fallen.'

Sometimes, Philip told himself, true intentions are misunderstood.

'I'm going to take this cat to the vet right now,' he said.

'Can I come?' said the child.

'No. Tell your parents I will have Muffin back in a jiffy,' said Philip.

He gathered the cat very carefully in his arms, placed it on his coat on the back seat of the car, and drove to the vet.

After a long afternoon in which he twice explained to the vet how, during the course of dusting, a book which sat on the window ledge had been nudged out the window, it was established that Muffin would live. Her shoulder had been dislocated, and the vet told Philip that it would take some time to heal and he'd have to bring her in regularly for check-ups.

Philip explained the story quietly to his neighbours. He said that he'd wished he'd listened to his wife when she'd told him not to leave things lying around. He said he would pay for any further medical attention the cat needed. Muffin licked his hand and gave a soft purr when he knelt down to pat her. The neighbours seemed soothed by their cat's actions, and although Philip felt his skin grow itchy he didn't let it show.

Literature

The equinoctial winds woke him just after midnight. A large stable of horses had escaped and were thrashing about the valley. Between the horses' hooves was the sound of Marilyn's deep breathing, a gentle but high-pitched whistle when she exhaled. He thought he heard one of the children call out in their sleep, but it was hard to tell over all the noise.

Philip gave up and opened his eyes. Light from the street lamps was leaking in through a gap in the curtains. The light hit Marilyn's face and he could see her, beautiful and concentrated in her sleep. Perhaps he gazed too intently, for she mumbled and turned away from him. He rose from the bed.

A trip to the zoo was planned for the morning and Philip had talked it up to the boys all week. Going to the zoo could never be a spontaneous decision. It was an activity that required a good night's rest. How Marilyn managed the two boys all week and still got to meetings and book club evenings was a mystery to him. Perhaps childbirth gave women a natural resilience.

Philip sat in his reading chair. The roof creaked and the gate at the side path rattled. The catch needed replacing. His life was full of lists and plans.

He opened the stiff cover of his library book. Though published ten years ago, the book looked barely read. From the first paragraph he knew he would like it. It was the sort of writing that made him feel the zoo excursion would be something easily conquered, even perhaps enjoyed. Philip and his good friend James sought out and shared such books. They gave each other maps to the small grails hidden in the public library.

He read for half an hour. Then his eyes closed and he slept, still upright in the chair. His mind galloped along wild valleys and over mountainous passes.

But then the sound of the northerly entered his dreams as a tornado. Bald monkeys bared their sharp incisors and stuffed birds clutching waxy apples swirled around him. What had seemed whimsical under the reading lamp in sleep was deathly. He dreamt that silver-feathered intruders were dragging his children out of their beds. When he tried to beat the intruders away, they dissolved and he was left clutching sticky feathers, his children staring at him with large and terrified eyes as if it was their father, not the birds, who had murderous intentions.

Philip woke in the early light to the boys shouting for their mother. Sleep had left him tattered, and not for the first time he wished a serious but non-fatal illness upon himself, something that put him in bed for a couple of weeks but still left him able to read.

He dressed the boys in their bathrobes, and poured cornflakes and milk into two bowls. He put a movie on and lay down on the sofa. Before the opening credits were over, Philip was drifting to sleep. Then he felt a small wind against his lip. The bald monkey was back, and it was touching him. He opened his eyes.

George was leaning over Philip's head, rubbing the mole on his throat.

'What's that?' George pressed his finger hard against the mole.

Philip batted the child's hand away. 'It's a mole, don't touch it.'

'Does it hurt?'

'It will if you keep touching it.'

'Why?'

'It just will. You shouldn't play with other people's moles.'

'Why?'

'Jake's grandpa died from a bad mole,' said Charlie.

They were all quiet for a moment.

'It grew bigger and it was bad and then he was dead,' said Charlie.

'Why did Jake's grandpa die?' said George.

'He got sick,' said Philip.

George turned back towards the TV. A fox was getting shot at.

'In a long, long, long time, when you die—'

Philip looked at the child.

'Who will make my dinner?'

16

'Well, that's a long, long, long time away,' said Philip.

George nodded seriously and waited for an answer.

'You will make your own dinner,' said Philip.

George's bottom lip started to stick out and he scrunched his eyes up. 'I can't make my dinner.'

Philip pulled him in for a hug. 'It's okay, honey, you don't need to think about it.' He stroked George's cheek. The skin was smooth and plump, and George smelt fresh; nothing in him had turned yet. Even the snot that ran down to his lip, and then shot back up into his nose when he sniffed, was clear. Philip wanted to say, I won't die, you won't die. You will never, ever have to make your own dinner.

As usual James was a little late and apologetic. His son, Thomas, arrived first. He shrieked when he saw George and flung his arms around him, muffling George's face with his wild hair. They ran down the path together, with Charlie following.

'How's the law office?' said James.

Philip shrugged. 'Ticking over. How are the lab rats?'

James gave a quick false smile. 'Stop pushing, Thomas,' he shouted towards the children's backs. 'One of the rats had a seizure yesterday. A student cried.' James rolled his eyes.

Philip and James had done philosophy together at university. Philip had also done a law degree and James neuroscience. He taught at the university now; his specialty area was fear and stress.

Philip felt the weight of the dream hanging over him and he started to tell James about it. James was good at interpreting stuff. Philip said he felt like the book had tapped into some deep anxiety.

'Well,' said James, 'that's what literature does, I suppose. Although I thought the book was less about anxiety than about our—'

A noise rang out that sounded like a cross between an animal attack and a car alarm.

'Christ,' said James.

Then Philip heard Charlie scream.

They ran.

Charlie and Thomas were standing in front of an enclosure, their faces pale. Behind a thick pane of glass two lemurs were sitting staring out at the boys. Philip held Charlie by the shoulders and examined him for damage. Nothing apparent showed.

'Um,' said James. 'Where's George?'

Thomas pointed.

George was sitting inside the enclosure. He had climbed on top of a large tree trunk above the lemurs. He waved.

Philip felt a rush of fear and adrenaline. He felt as though he'd been swallowed back into his dream. The lemurs looked up at George, then back at Philip, seeing instantly the connection between the two males. Philip felt their cold animal eyes bore into his heart and see the frailties there. They were small creatures, but he saw that in an instant they could break the child.

'Fuck,' said James.

Philip didn't take his eyes off the lemurs. 'Go and get some help,' he said. 'Go!'

Philip waited. He waited, and the sun moved across the sky and went down on the other side. He waited, and the tired, broken moon came up. The grey at Philip's temples

18

spread up to the crown of his head until his hair was bleached to silvery white. Above them the night sky was clear and the stars made tiny sharp points of light. The lemurs looked up at those foreign stars and they howled. The howl was a siren and it rang through the valley. It was a song and it named the trees and the lake where they came from; it named their parents and their parents' parents. It was a ballad of ghosts and loss. All the while, George slept curled in the tree.

And, when the help arrived, the lemurs handed George back, sleepy and unscathed. Once more they turned their animal eyes on Philip, and he saw that they were just as scared as he was.

The Yellow Scarf

Lukas sat at his desk in the reception of Philip's office. He hollered at Philip and whistled a long appreciative note.

'Get a load of this,' he said.

Philip sighed, and went and stood in his doorway. Lukas held out a bit of fabric for him to touch.

'Now that's real cashmere,' said Lukas.

It was a lemony yellow and still partly wrapped in Harrod's tissue paper. Philip touched the scarf lightly.

'Rick, eh,' he said. 'He remembered his pater after all.'

'A bit late,' said Lukas. He rubbed the scarf against his cheek. 'It's a busy time for financiers. That's what he says in the note.'

Lukas thrust a small card at Philip, a picture of an English cottage garden. Philip turned it over and read Rick's usual brief scrawl. Lukas unwrapped the scarf and threw it round his thin throat with a flourish.

'A bit of colour does a lot for an old joker like me. You could do with some colour yourself, boss,' he said.

Lukas had started to dress more flamboyantly after his wife died, sometimes wearing a fedora at a natty angle, but his general pallor was grey and his suits hung off his bony shoulders. He had to keep getting his trousers taken in. Once, he'd lifted his shirt to show Philip how his belt sat loose on his hips. Philip had caught sight of the large purple scar beneath Lukas's navel.

When nervous young couples making first house purchases came into the office, Lukas would smooth his hands over his thin hair and straighten his jacket.

'Philip will see you right,' he would tell them. 'He won't rip you off like those firms in the city.' He'd wink as he saw them into Philip's office. 'Do you like my tie? I don't dress this well in the weekends.'

Now Lukas was playing with the yellow scarf around his neck, knotting it at the front.

'Loose or tied?' he said.

Philip shrugged.

'Oh, come on, boss. You don't know who you'll meet in town.'

'Loose, I guess,' said Philip.

'Yep. That's what I thought,' said Lukas. 'Here's our man.'

Stan appeared in the doorway. Philip raised a hand in greeting.

'Do you lot ever do any work?' said Stan.

Lukas rubbed his scarf. 'The boss has just been admiring my new cashmere scarf,' he said.

Stan smiled. 'Where'd you nick that from, young fulla?' he said.

'A gift from my Rick,' said Lukas. 'Not too busy to remember his old man after all. Now, we have a luncheon to get to, don't we Stanley? Stop your chatter and let's move.'

Lukas walked slowly over to the door. Philip waved them both goodbye.

It was Lukas and Stan's Friday ritual to go into town for 'num char'. That's what Lukas called it. Num char was a highlight in Lukas's week, even though he had trouble digesting food properly now. Stan called Lukas a cheap date. Lukas called Stan a ladies' man. It was a bit of a standing joke between them. Stan had been married three times.

'No luck with the wives, our Stanley,' Lukas told Philip once. 'First wife was a terrible depressive.'

Stan was a client. He'd been a client of Lukas's late wife Gin and had stayed on after Philip bought the office. Philip had done the divorce proceedings for Stan's third marriage. Stan had been generous with the payout, though they'd had no children. He'd left his wife a freehold house. Stan owned a number of properties around town and wasn't short of cash, but Philip questioned him on his decision to give up the whole house. Stan just shook his head and said, 'I have no choice, mate. Women, eh.' His face was drawn and he kept his eyes down, so Philip didn't push him any further. Lukas told him that Stan said he'd never marry again, that he was done with women. Most of the time when Stan dropped into the office they talked about the weather or the rugby.

'Friday lunches,' Philip said to Stan one day, 'mean a lot to Lukas.'

Stan waved his hand a little. 'I don't think it does the old gut much good though.'

'You'd have to tie him to a train track before he'd admit it,' said Philip.

The trouble with the trust account went unnoticed by Philip until the Law Society secretary phoned one Friday afternoon. Lukas had gone home early with a stomach ache. The accounts hadn't balanced last month and Lukas had not contacted the society to say why. The secretary said that it was only a matter of twenty-odd dollars but that they couldn't break the rules. Philip heard himself making excuses for Lukas. His voice sounded weak. The secretary told him that an auditor would be in first thing next week.

When Lukas arrived at work on Monday, Philip wasn't sure how to mention the auditor. He was still thinking about it when she arrived. She held out a thin hand and introduced herself as Anna. She wore a well-cut dark suit. Lukas, sitting at his desk in reception, didn't ask any questions, but he set his face in a scowl and spread his pen and pad further out on his desk. Philip showed Anna through to the spare office.

The room smelt stale, and the old Greek islands tourism poster on the wall had faded. It had been Lukas's office until Gin's death. Philip wished he'd thought to open a window. Anna looked around at the bare shelves. Philip wanted to make light of the obvious lack of cleaning, but didn't want Lukas to hear him apologising. He arranged a chair at the desk and pulled the top draw open.

'There are pens in here, if you need them,' said Philip.

'I just need to access your accounts. We bring our own stationery,' said Anna.

Philip handed her the ledger book. She turned it over in her hands, as if to ask where the rest of it was.

'I guess you'll need the client account cards, too, when you get to that part.' He pointed through the window at the small grey box behind Lukas, who glared at Philip and Anna.

'Is everything done manually?' she said.

'Yes,' said Philip, 'that's the way Lukas has always done it.'

Anna nodded. Philip detected a faint sigh.

'Cup of tea?' he said.

Lukas followed Philip out to the kitchen and stood right beside him while he put the kettle on.

'I suppose you'll be offering her our biscuits as well,' said Lukas.

'That would be nice,' said Philip.

A supply of malts was kept in a tin for morning tea. Lukas would offer them to clients he particularly liked. He'd told Philip that times would have to be really tough before they stopped buying malts.

Lukas gave a slight grunt. 'None for me,' he said. He reached for the tin and passed it to Philip. 'Shame for a good-looking lass like her to be doing such a job.'

'What do you mean, Lukas?'

'They're the enemy,' he whispered. It almost sounded like a hiss.

Philip wanted to laugh, but he saw that Lukas was serious.

Lukas made a sharp intake of breath and clutched at his side. Philip looked at him.

'Oh. Don't worry about me. Just a bit of stress,' said Lukas. 'I think I'll go down to the caff now. The air's got stuffy in here.'

Philip thought that Lukas had been too well looked after by Gin. A few months after her death he had gone to visit Lukas at home. Lukas had shown Philip though to the kitchen and offered him a cup of tea. Dirty plates with dried baked beans were stacked high on the bench and the place had a slight fishy smell.

Lukas put his nose in the milk bottle. 'You don't mind taking it black, do you?' He pushed some envelopes and files to a corner of the table to clear a space.

'Here's a picture of Rick's wee one.' He gave Philip a photo of a tiny baby, its eyes still closed. 'I wish he'd marry the mother. A baby needs a mother, don't you think?'

'Well, these days—'

'Pah. These days.' Lukas slurped at his tea. 'You've done those messy settlements. A child needs to know its place in the world, needs some legitimacy. Rick doesn't get that. I love the boy but, you know, he's crazy. He's always chasing after the next thing. No sticking power. His mother said it was from my side, but look at me. Still in the same house we got married in. Still got the same blasted wallpaper. I never played around, not once, even when I had the chance.'

'Well, the law has changed a lot in the last few years.'

'Rick's mother would turn in her grave. She was all for feminine rights and that lot.' Lukas looked out the window to where the grass was almost knee height. 'She didn't even get to meet her own granddaughter.'

'Does Rick say he might come over?'

'In the summer.' Lukas looked at Philip. 'I'll get to meet the little heiress in the summer. All this will be hers. It's not like Rick needs it.'

Last year, Lukas had told Philip that Rick made four million in bonuses. Pounds, he said. Lukas had spat the number out like a bad taste.

Philip excused himself to the toilet.

'It's where it was last time you came,' Lukas called out after him.

The toilet bowl was grimy and the cistern seemed to be making a small squeaking sound. Philip hit it a couple of times, but the squeak continued. Then he realised the sound was coming from within the wall. He put the lid down and followed the noise to a cupboard in the hall.

Nestled in some towels and sheets was a cat with five kittens. The cat gave a low growl and moved further back into the recess. The kittens pushed over one another to move closer to their mother.

'Hey,' Philip called out to Lukas. 'You've got a whole family in here.'

'That's Duster.' Lukas called out from the kitchen. 'I'm thinking of changing his name.'

Philip walked back into the kitchen and stood in the doorway.

'What are you going to do with them?'

'What do you mean? You want one?'

'You can't keep them all.'

Lukas didn't say anything. He didn't look at Philip.

'They don't stay that small for ever,' said Philip. He wanted to go back and shut the cupboard door and pretend he hadn't seen them. 'I mean, Duster won't take care of them much longer.'

'We'll cross that bridge when we get to it, won't we,' said Lukas. He looked down at the pile of envelopes and put the photo back into one. Philip watched him move some papers around on the table.

Philip arranged for his cleaner to come fortnightly to Lukas's. Lukas protested until Philip mentioned that the cost would be subsidised because of his health and circumstances. He also arranged for some meals to be dropped off to him three times a week. He wasn't sure that Lukas knew how to cook anything.

Anna stayed at the office all week. She was polite but barely spoke to them, and made all her phone calls on her mobile, with her back turned to the office. Philip offered her a cup of tea whenever he made one for himself. Mostly she declined.

On Thursday afternoon, as she said goodbye for the day, Philip asked her how she was getting on. She looked him in the eye and her face softened.

'It's quite a tangle in there,' she said.

Philip wasn't worried about the trust account. He knew there was no intent on Lukas's part to swindle money. But the call from the Law Society had unsettled him. He hadn't noticed that Lukas was having difficulty, and Lukas had told him nothing.

By Friday morning Philip didn't want to go to work. The thought of Lukas sitting and scribbling on his desk pad irritated him. At least Stan would be along to take Lukas out to lunch. That would help his mood a little.

But when Philip came back from his lunch on Friday, Lukas was still at his desk. He had an empty, pitiful sort of look on his face.

'No Stan?' Philip said.

'It seems he is otherwise engaged,' said Lukas.

'Did you phone him?'

Lukas nodded and gave one of his sharp intakes of breath. 'He's a dark horse is our Stanley. A dark horse.'

Philip thought Lukas meant to imply that Stan had a new lady in his life. This kind of development would bump Lukas down on Stan's list. Philip pictured the empty house that Lukas would be returning to. And he'd missed out on his lunch. The week had treated him hard. A wave of guilt and pity came over him, and he asked Lukas if he wanted to join them for greasies that night. He knew Marilyn would be annoyed, as would Charlie and George who complained that Lukas looked at them mean.

Lukas shook his head. 'My appetite seems to have left me.' He looked up at Philip. 'Thanks, boss. I'll be off now.'

Lukas often made a show of putting his long tailored coat on. If it was particularly cold he might wear the old brown trilby he kept at the office. Today he just shrugged his coat over his thin shoulders.

'Did you know,' said Lukas, 'Stan had a son once.'

Philip looked up.

'He hung himself.'

'Dear God,' said Philip.

'Stan found the body. Wouldn't know it to look at him, would you?' said Lukas.

Philip wasn't sure what that man would look like. There was nothing unexpected about Stan. Perhaps that was why, thought Philip. That's how a person became like Stan: they squash themselves down and down, until there's nothing particularly noticeable about them.

'There are many quiet tragedies in this world,' said Lukas. He looked through at Anna. She had her back turned to them and was on her mobile. 'That's something herself in there has yet to learn,' he said.

Philip didn't respond. He felt relieved that Lukas had declined the offer of dinner. He was tired, and he wanted a rest from thinking about him. Plus he had a cross-lease title to check over by four o'clock.

'Are you sure you won't come for tea?' said Philip.

'Nah.' Lukas gave Philip a slow wave. 'See you Monday, boss.'

Philip heard Lukas pick up the mail on his way out.

'You're a good decent man, Philip,' he called.

Philip knew he meant to point out that Anna wasn't of the same class.

For half an hour Philip worked at the contract. He forgot about Lukas and Anna next door until he heard her standing just outside his office.

'Can I talk to you for a minute? I need to show you something,' said Anna.

He followed her through to the spare room. She pointed at a page from June the year before. The page was a mess. Columns with numbers crossed out, and new figures drawn over time and time again as if to state their permanence, their right place in the book.

'You can see here,' she said. She followed a few lines of figures with her finger. 'He's only a few cents out, but you carry that over and . . . You can see where he's tried to correct himself. But—' she shook her head '—these numbers don't add up.' She looked at Philip. 'Everyone makes mistakes. But it's like he sort of got lost.'

Philip was aware that the end-of-month accounts had been starting earlier and were taking Lukas longer. He'd put this down to him being tired—Lukas often complained that the pills he had to take made him sleepy. Philip thought now that this was a failure on his own part. He'd worried about Lukas to the point of insomnia after Gin's death, but over the past few months he'd fallen into a state of inattention around him. Philip knew his complacency was because he didn't know what to do with him.

'I'll have to talk to him about this.' Philip spoke out loud, but he was talking to himself.

Anna made a small noise in her throat.

'I just wondered, is he unwell? He makes these sounds every now and then. He doesn't sound right,' she said.

'He's missing half his stomach. Cancer.'

'Oh.'

'And he's old,' said Philip.

Anna nodded. 'It must be hard, I imagine, for you.' She blushed a little. 'I mean. You're very kind to him.'

'You mean he's a grumpy old man that I put up with.' Philip felt pissed off. At Anna, at Lukas. At Stan for not even ringing to cancel lunch.

'I didn't mean it like that.' She went red. 'I'm sorry.'

'I need to finish this contract. Thanks for showing me. It's not your fault. He didn't used to be like this,' said Philip.

Philip went back to his office and sat down in his chair. Looking around, he could see that the place looked as worn as he felt. He would have to get in help. Someone to answer the phone and help Lukas out. Slowly Lukas could hand over the books and teach them what to do. But that was hopeless. Who could learn from Lukas? One day, he thought, someone will think the same thing about me.

He was wondering how to start talking to Lukas when there was a knock at the front door. A man in a dark navy suit stood outside. He was accompanied by a more casually dressed man in smart denims.

'Philip Fetch?'

Philip knew they were police. He nodded.

'I'm Detective Inspector Morris, this is Constable Warwick.' The detective held out his hand.

Philip shook his hand and motioned them into the office. He looked in at Anna. She looked away and coughed politely. Philip made sure his office door was shut firmly behind them. As he sat down he could feel his pulse speeding, but he also felt strangely deflated and wanted to slump in his chair like a sulky teenager. Perhaps he'd completely underestimated Lukas's state of mind.

'We'll come straight to it, Mr Fetch,' said the detective. 'A body was found at the old paint factory this morning.'

Philip felt a fleeting relief. Lukas had left at two, so the body couldn't be his.

The detective cleared his throat. 'It has been identified as Stanley Patterson. The body was somewhat . . . disfigured.'

He looked closely at Philip to gauge his reaction.

'Christ,' said Phillip.

'When did you last see Mr Patterson?' said the detective.

Both he and the constable looked straight at Philip.

Philip sat back in his chair. He knew he couldn't possibly be a suspect if this was murder. But then Stan was hardly the type he'd expect to be found dead at a factory, disfigured.

'Last Friday. Stan takes Lukas to lunch every Friday,' he said.

Philip wondered what they meant by disfigured. He kept seeing a picture of Stan standing by his own son's dead and hanging body.

'Is Lukas a work colleague?' said the detective.

'Lukas is—' Philip couldn't think what to call Lukas, what professional title to give him. He'd always struggled with that and now, in light of Anna sitting next door, he could hardly call him an accountant. 'Lukas helps out around the office,' he said.

'Are you Stanley Patterson's lawyer?' said the constable.

Philip nodded.

'Do you hold his will?'

'Yes. I did his estate and any conveyancing for him. Stan did a bit of property development,' said Philip.

'Stanley Patterson purchased a number of properties over the last five years,' said the detective.

'Yes. Around eight, maybe nine? We did all the work for him. He's a loyal client.' Philip paused. 'Was a loyal client.'

The detective gave Philip a long look. 'Where do you think a retired ambulance driver would get money for ten properties?' he said.

Philip had never mentioned it to Lukas, but he'd always thought Stan had won Lotto at some stage and had just kept silent about it. Philip realised that he had papered over a hole in his knowledge. It had never seemed that important to know. And now Philip felt as if some murky water had entered his body; some tarnished matter was swimming inside of him. He was exhausted, and he wanted to lie down on the carpet and sleep.

'Stan was murdered?' he said. His voice felt very far removed from his thoughts.

'We are unable to comment at this stage, Mr Fetch,' said the constable.

'His head was severed and found a few metres from his body. There was an attempt made to sever the hands as well,' said the detective.

For a moment Philip thought he might be sick. Why were they telling him all this? Was it some sort of police test? If they suspected him they should be taking him down to the station. He felt like he might be in a TV show.

'It's very hard to sever hands. You'd need one of those Japanese swords. What are they called?' said the constable.

'Samurai,' said Philip quietly.

'Yes,' said the constable. 'That's it. The Japanese are very good with steel. I read an article about it once.'

The detective cut in. 'Obviously, we are investigating. As his lawyer, we thought you might know who he dealt with on a regular basis.'

'I don't . . .' said Philip, and stopped. He realised he knew nothing about Stan. The Stan he thought he knew was a man with a bit of money; a kind man with a bit of spare change.

Stan came to Philip with work because he liked him. He took Lukas out to lunch because Lukas was his friend. Stan wore brown workpants and plain shirts. The only embellished thing about him was his gold belt buckle with decorative deer horns—a gift from his girlfriend, he'd said one day with an embarrassed look.

The detective asked him a few more questions and Philip showed him Stan's will. They asked for his phone number so they could phone him on the weekend if they needed to. They thanked him for his help and left.

Philip slumped in his chair and put his head in his hands. He felt he wanted to sob. After a while he heard Anna making small shuffling sounds. He looked up and saw her standing in the doorway.

'Are you okay?' she said.

Philip took a deep breath and shrugged.

'The walls are very thin here,' she said.

'It doesn't matter,' said Philip.

'Was he a good friend of yours, this man?'

Philip wondered himself. 'A friend?' he said.

Without warning a large wail came from deep in his chest, the sort of cry he'd expect from George. Anna stood still and bit her lip.

'Would you like a cup of tea?' she said.

Philip wiped his face and nodded. 'Sorry,' he said.

The tea she brought to him was hot and strong. Anna sat in the chair opposite his and sipped her drink. She was silent for a long while. Philip was grateful for this and didn't want her to leave. They both looked out the window. The glass was covered in a fine grey film because Philip was unsure who to phone to clean the high windows.

'I've never known a murdered person,' said Anna after a while.

'Me neither,' said Philip.

Then Anna stretched her hand across his desk and placed it on his. Her hand was warm and soft, and for the first time Philip noticed she wore a wedding band.

'I think you are a very kind man, Philip,' she said.

He looked at her as she spoke and he saw that her eyes were distinctly blue. He felt that if he was the sort of man to do such a thing he might fall in love with her.

But he wasn't, so he nodded to say thank you and then looked away. He didn't want her to see him cry again. She knew this and removed her hand, but she sat in the chair for a while longer.

Three months after Stan's body was found, Lukas died. He'd been admitted to hospital and put on a drip, no longer able to eat. His cancer had returned. Sitting in the hospital bed, Lukas took the scarf from around his neck and held it out to Philip.

'I think you'd look good in this,' said Lukas.

Philip put it on. It was warm from Lukas wearing it.

'You see.' Lukas smiled. 'The nurses won't let you out of the building now.'

Philip had broken the news about Stan's death in Lukas's living room with Trackside TV playing in the corner. Lukas had looked quickly away from Philip and back to the horses. His mouth hung open slightly as though it had somehow come unhinged.

They watched a race together, not speaking or even urging the horses on.

When it had finished, Lukas said, 'I don't believe you.' He shook his head and wiped the corner of his mouth with his shirtsleeve. 'You shouldn't tell lies, Philip Fetch. Stanley is a good man.'

Philip didn't try to convince him otherwise. Soon Lukas would turn on the news and he'd see a picture of Stan on the telly. Philip understood that they would never speak of Stan again.

Philip wore the scarf to Lukas's funeral. He spoke at the service about his friend and how he would miss him at work. In the tearooms at the church, Lukas's son Rick put a glass of whisky in his hand and pointed at the scarf.

'I'm glad to see someone appreciates cashmere. Lucinda, my girlfriend, she bought it. I told her it wouldn't be Dad's thing.' Rick gave a little snort. 'He despised anything showy.'

'Tell Lucinda that your father loved it,' said Philip.

'Dad? Ha!'

They looked away from each other.

Attendance at the funeral was small but respectable. Many of Lukas's friends were in homes or had moved away. They had sent their condolences to the law office. Philip was surprised to see Anna at the service. They'd waved at each other, but not had a chance to speak.

'You don't know, do you,' said Rick, 'who that girl over there is?'

He pointed at Anna, and at that moment Philip felt he might punch Rick, just lightly, in the guts.

Anna noticed them looking, and walked over.

'Hi, Philip,' she said, and smiled.

He smiled back. 'Anna, this is Rick. Lukas's son.'

Rick held out his hand. 'A pleasure,' he said. He gave Anna a smile, which Philip thought made him seem a bit too sure of himself.

'Unfortunately, Rick's partner and daughter couldn't make it,' said Philip.

'Oh, that's a pity,' she said. 'I'm so sorry for your loss. I only met your father briefly. He was funny.'

Then she turned to Philip in such a way that Rick was excluded.

'Are you doing okay?' she said quietly. And now she held his arm. 'I wanted to ring you but I didn't want to seem, you know, prying.' Her cheeks reddened a little. 'It was such a strange week, wasn't it?'

'I'll just go and refresh my drink,' said Rick.

'Found any fraudsters recently?' Philip asked.

'Don't you know?' Anna said. 'I've left the Law Society. I'm going to New York next week. Things didn't quite work out between me and my husband.' She corrected herself. 'Ex-husband.' Philip watched her eyes brighten. 'So I'm making a break.'

'Well, that's great,' said Philip. He felt old.

'If I hadn't had that week at your office—' Anna shook her head '—with that guy getting murdered and everything. It kind of made me realise that I had to do something else.'

Philip took a large sip of his whisky. He felt it burn all the way down his throat to his stomach.

They spoke for a few minutes about New York and the

38

art galleries there, and Philip said he'd never been but he'd like to. Anna chatted to him about her plans, and her eyes were lively. Philip watched her talking but didn't hear a thing. Their conversation dwindled to a stop.

'Well,' she said.

'Have fun in New York,' he said.

She leaned towards him and whispered. 'Thank you, Philip Fetch.'

Her hair tickled his cheek. He watched her move out the door and felt his arms heavy at his side.

Out the window, Philip thought he saw the hem of Anna's coat disappear around the corner, but it was almost dark and when he blinked and looked again it was just himself and the room behind him that he could see reflected in the glass. He looked tired. As if to make reparations, he smoothed the yellow scarf around his neck a little. Lukas was right. A bit of colour might do him good.

Lunar Conversations

They were standing out under the dead sun when he saw her. Philip saw his mother where the sun's face had been only a minute ago, and he said, 'Holy mother of Christ.'

'Mind your tongue,' she said.

No one took any notice of them. The boys had their little foil-covered shoeboxes pressed hard against their faces and they were making a drama out of the whole thing. James had warned them not to look at the eclipse directly unless they wanted to burn out their retinas. They'd grabbed hold of this bit of information and were milking it.

'Ahh!' said Charlie, and staggered a few times before falling to the ground with his hands over his face. 'My eyes are bleeding, my eyes are bleeding!'

George, who found most things his older brother did hilarious, copied him.

'Mum?' said Philip.

'Who else would I b-be? D-D-Dusty Springfield?' she said. Even dead, his mother's stammer still hung around.

James was huddled over his recording box, not even looking up but fiddling with one of the reels of tape that kept getting stuck in the machine. His earphones were clamped tight, so maybe he couldn't hear Philip.

'You've b-been indulging,' she said, and patted her middle.

Philip put his own hand on his thickening waist. He meant to get out on the bike more, but . . .

He squinted at her. It was hard to make out—the darkening sky had made him a bit blind—but he thought she had on her blue suit. The one with the permanent press that she saved for funerals.

'Have a piece of tan square.' His mother stretched her arm, if that's what you could call it, towards him. A hand extended from the sky. Philip blinked, but out of polite habit he reached forward. A cool slap, like a strong gust of wind, knocked his hand back.

'Not that piece, that's for Robyn,' she said.

'Robyn's in London,' said Philip. He gave a small cough. 'Mother, are you, um, in heaven?'

'No. I'm right here,' she said. She gave a little wave, like a queen waving from her coach.

At this point he had to look away, as if the rust of the eclipse was infecting his eyes. She was changed. She was not his mother, but someone like her. She was a shadow without a form to cast it. He blinked and looked again.

'You look like your father,' she said. 'You're a bit s-softer, though. He was like a bull at your age. Just couldn't wait.'

Philip was unsure what to make of this.

She gave a loud sigh. 'Where's Robyn?' she said, looking around. 'She's going to be late.'

'Philip! Are you deaf?' James called him over. 'I've been yelling at you. I'm getting something,' he said. 'Listen.' He handed Philip the headphones.

James had shown Philip diagrams, explained how the moment of eclipse had a pitch not discernible to human ears. The area of frequency transduction was not new, but improvements were being made all the time, he said. His aim was to capture it. The pictures James drew made no sense to Philip, but he went along for the ride.

He put the headphones on and heard a crackle. Then his mother's voice boomed into his ears.

'What the hell are you doing?' she said. 'And what's that smell? Like a b-bloody cow shed down there.'

Philip turned quickly to James to see if he'd heard her, and knocked an aerial off the box.

'Watch out,' said his mother. 'That stuff looks expensive.'

James rolled his eyes. 'Give me the headphones,' he said.

Philip handed them back. 'Did you hear that?' he said.

'Not sure. Something's coming through,' said James. 'Mainly static.'

Philip gave a small nod. 'Yeah,' he said, 'static.'

'Who are those small p-people?' said his mother.

'They're my sons, Charlie and George.' It felt good to say their names, their living, breathing names.

'That one's got my cheekbones,' she said.

'You want to meet them?' said Philip.

'Don't be stupid, they can't see me. You're the uh-uh-only one, Philip dear. Just you.' A slit of light appeared at her side as if a door to a bright room had been left ajar. 'Tell Robyn I'm upset she was s-s-so late.'

There was a sound like waves rolling back off a pebbled shore, and his mother's face disappeared.

'I . . .' said Philip.

James was huddled over the back of his machine, playing with some wires.

Philip looked up.

There was a strange glow about the sky now. Looking at it, Philip felt himself lighten, as if he might be lifted into that strange celestial theatre and become a part of its atomic vibration. The moon and sun were constantly turning even though they didn't seem to. The whole world, in all its blindness and denial, was always moving.

'I don't know where your sister could have g-g-got to.' His mother's voice seemed to come from under water.

She's in bloody London! Philip went to shout, but when he opened his mouth nothing came out. He saw his mother was being erased by light. Her shadow was turning to vapour. Philip felt as though he was bathing in a warm and silky void. He was falling into the sun, and it felt wonderful. He was falling.

'No!' shouted Philip.

He fell to his knees on the damp grass. Above him the sun was out, alive and well again, and the moon was fading away. James was packing up his tapes and aerials. The kids had wandered out of sight, their silver viewing boxes abandoned on the grass.

The Plastic City

Some things in Philip's life caused him great anguish. He was aware of the disparity between the size of the thing and the feeling it aroused, but he was also someone who knew the universe to be an interconnected place: moon to the waves and rhythms of the world; house paint to the toxic red bloom in the bay.

It was a time when people were concerned about the world but were flailing. Philip and James liked to read around the subject. James's car ran on vegetable oil that he collected from local fish and chip shops. A system of ropes and pulleys, pipes and tanks attached to the outside of his house collected rainwater for drinking.

After visiting James, Philip would come back determined to safe-fast his home. It was his duty to his wife and children. Indeed, small-scale changes had a ripple-out effect. He could shake the world. From his chair at the dining table, he could see there was a lot of work to be done.

'Do you think there's lead paint on our window sills?' Philip asked Marilyn. He had read that houses of a certain age probably had it.

Marilyn was cooking dinner. 'Uh, maybe,' she shrugged.

'This winter we should insulate the house,' said Philip. 'I read about this type of natural fleece. You know, sheep wool.'

'Yes.'

'Yes, and I wondered about these German radiators. They run off solar panels.'

'How much work have you got on right now?' said Marilyn.

'Ah,' said Philip. Things had slowed down a little. 'I could get a book from the library. Do some of this stuff myself.'

Marilyn stopped reading a recipe and looked at him.

'What?' he said.

She looked down at the recipe again.

'Yeah, I know.' He looked out the window. 'It's just that I want to do something. You know, do it myself.'

She leaned her hip against the kitchen bench and smiled. 'Yes. But that's why you do law, so that we can pay other people to do insulation and radiators.' She took a sip of her beer and smiled. 'Can you get the mixing bowl down?' she said.

Philip wished he could better explain himself. In conversation, his thoughts tended to burst their dam. Ideas didn't arrive in an orderly fashion.

He stood on a chair and reached up into the high cupboard. The mixing bowl was hidden behind a huge stack of plastic containers. As he pulled the bowl forward, some containers tumbled out of the cupboard and onto the floor.

'Damn. I've been meaning to clear them,' said Marilyn.

'That's a lot of containers.' Philip tried not to sound annoyed. He was tired and had been looking forward to sitting down with a quiet beer. He handed her the bowl and stacked the containers back into their cupboard.

After the children had gone to bed, Philip did some research on the internet. Like the supermarket, the internet has a way of stunning those who come without written notes to guide them. They get stuck in an aisle, eyes blinking under the fluorescent lights, grabbing products they don't need, intentions forgotten.

Philip read about the antioxidant properties in blackcurrants and new discoveries indicating the importance of eating animal fats. His eyes darted around the screen, picking up facts and sound-bites to pass on to Marilyn.

Then, lured by the title 'Common items poisoning your family', Philip followed a link. It turned out these poisonous things were everywhere: in clothing and glues, paints and waxes, plastics, curtain backings and moisturisers, liquid soaps and toys. Already, Europe was banning them.

Philip looked around him. It was worse than he thought. He lifted his hands off the keyboard suspiciously. It was a comfort to climb into bed that night and hold his book and breathe its papery scent. It almost smelt like a forest to Philip.

It was no wonder, then, that he woke at three in the morning, the hour that presents the most trouble in the twenty-four-hour cycle of the anxious. But instead of turning his worries back and forward like a Rubik's Cube, Philip got up and went to the kitchen.

He climbed up into the cupboard and began to pull out all the plastic containers. Yoghurt pottles, ice-cream boxes, hummus and olive tubs, salad oil and water bottles—all spread out over the kitchen floor. He opened the pantry door. Another world of toxic aggressors resided there. He gathered as many glass bottling jars as he could find, and decanted sugars and coconut, spices and peppercorns and biscuits out of their plastic holdings. The rest he threw away, convinced now that it would be better to start afresh. He opened the drawers and gathered up the plastic wrap and all the little ice-cream spoons that the children collected, even their favourite drinking cups and straws. Philip stacked them in chaotic piles on the floor.

Around him a plastic city grew. Towers of transparent pottles, pyramids of tubs, their blue and green lids lending them a watery, skyish colour. After a solid half hour of work, Philip sat on his chair and gazed at the towering city. It was a monster. It had grown without thought or planning. People had somehow come to accept that these flimsy little pots, their endocrine-altering possibilities obscured, were the way of the future. The plastic city had fooled them with its convenience and promises of long life.

An ache spread through Philip's body. He wanted to roar, but the family were sleeping. Instead, he bagged up the plastics and took them down to the shed.

The next morning Marilyn asked Philip if he'd seen the children's lunchboxes.

'I'm sure I put them in the dishwasher,' said Marilyn.

'I had an epiphany in the night,' said Philip.

Upon hearing that his lunchbox was gone, George started to cry.

'But will we have lunch today, Mummy?' he said. His voice had a quaver of fear in it.

'For Christ's sake, Philip. I'm pleased you want to save us from plastic. But what am I supposed to put anything in?' said Marilyn.

Philip felt the determination he'd had in the dark hours leak away a little. But he stopped himself from sinking further. He would soldier on.

'Small beginnings,' he said with a bright smile. He patted George on the head and gave Marilyn a kiss. 'We shall make do.'

Philip cleared Marilyn's wooden jewellery box and an old cigar box he'd kept tinnies in, when he used to do that sort of thing. He packed the children's sandwiches, wrapped in some muslin cloth he'd found in the laundry.

He gave the boys their new lunchboxes and they held them in their hands like foreign objects. Philip didn't let that get to him. He told them they'd all work on a new jewellery box to give to Marilyn for Mother's Day.

He walked the children to school. There were all the other parents and children starting out for the day, and he waved and called out his greetings as he passed. The day was fresh and George's small hand was warm in his. He was delivering the future of the world, and he would keep it safe.

Laughing Stock

Marilyn and Philip received a small, tasteful party invitation in the mail. It was from an old school friend of Marilyn's who had recently returned from overseas.

Philip did not want to go.

'Aside from everything else,' he said, 'her husband defended a mining business that let cyanide into a river. Didn't he also defend a former African dictator?'

Marilyn put the invitation down on the table and looked at him.

'Why would I want to go to his house?' said Philip.

'He doesn't work there any more. And I don't think he did the actual defence for those people, not directly,' she said.

'But how could you work for a company that defends toxic pollution and massacres?' said Philip.

Marilyn shrugged. 'It's murky, I know. I suppose someone

has to be the defence. Someone has to be for the bad guy.'

She was shuffling the mail, her head down.

'Yes, but it's a choice, right? We make choices every day. I don't wake up and think, Righto, today's the day I'm going to pillage my neighbour, do I? No, I say—not today, I'll wait until the weather's warmer.'

She gave a long sigh. 'That doesn't even make sense. Pamela is—' she paused a bit '—she's an old friend. I don't suppose it's been a walk in the park for her, living with a man like Hamish.' She looked down again when she said that.

'Well, I suppose someone had to,' he said.

'I'm going to go to the party, okay?' she said. 'You can come or not come.'

And she would go. He knew that. Marilyn was good at parties. She had a soft glow about her that quietly attracted people. Philip would stand beside his wife and make his own small gestures. After a while he'd feel that he was weighing her down, clouding her grace. He'd remove himself to a quiet room that would, with luck, have a magazine to flick through (a book was an obvious sign of failure) and try to look self-contained.

Pamela and Hamish's would be full of barristers and men with thickly rimmed glasses that indicated they were designers, even a real artist or two. Philip was none of these. Each of his clients had the sum total of his or her business with Philip written on a small card tucked alphabetically inside a grey metal box. He'd felt a quiet pride the day he'd had to acquire a second grey box; the housing market was on the rise, and word had got around that Philip did the job and didn't charge like a wounded bull.

He took a deep breath.

'Of course I'll go to the party,' he said.

Pamela and Hamish's house was in the nicer part of the valley—older houses with large grounds that were maintained by working gardeners. These homes occasionally featured in magazines. The photos showed thin women with drawn smiles and sometimes their husbands too, terriers at their feet. In private, the owners of these houses had plenty to complain about. There were the exposed beams and stair railings that were always dusty and impossible to reach (not that they ever cleaned them, but their help had trouble), and the floorboards ceaselessly creaked. Philip found this out as Pamela showed him and Marilyn in.

'Of course I'd never say it to anyone,' said Pamela. 'But sometimes we think it would be better to live in a new house.' She flicked her glance at Philip. 'Like you.'

Philip said that their house was built in the sixties, so it wasn't really new.

Pamela waved her hand. 'Oh, you know what I mean. Everything here is new compared to the Continent.'

'The Continent,' repeated Philip.

Marilyn pinched him lightly on the arm.

Pamela placed their coats in a cloakroom that had a strong smell of leather and perfume. She swung around to face them, and her eyes were shiny and electric.

'Don's here,' she said softly. She smiled with her lips partly open. Philip had to look away.

'Oh,' said Marilyn. 'Who's . . .'

'Shall we?' said Pamela, and she turned into a wide hallway.

Marilyn raised her eyebrows at Philip. He shrugged and trailed the two women slowly.

Art lined the hall; paintings and sketches crammed every space. He stopped in front of one, a black canvas with white writing, immediately recognisable. He read the words 'do not be over-righteous and do not be over-wise. Why make yourself a laughing stock?'

'Is that a—?' he said.

Pamela turned and gave a quick nod. 'But we're not here to look at that, not tonight,' she said, and pulled on his arm.

He moved reluctantly.

The party was at the end of the hall. He could hear it—a loud hum, a hive of talk and twitter. Philip's stomach tightened.

At the entrance, Pamela pointed over the many heads to the opposite corner. There was a string quartet playing on a slightly raised stage. He could see one player plucking his cello with a concentrated face.

'They're just back from an American tour,' she said.

He nodded. 'Very good.' He didn't know who they were. He caught snatches of the music, but it was mostly drowned out by the talk. People were laughing brightly. They held their drinks and leaned in close to one another, both to hear and to guard what was being said. Their eyes darted constantly around the room, checking who was there, and who wasn't.

He took a glass of red wine from a young woman who gestured her tray at him.

'Thank you,' he said, and gave a smile that showed he wasn't like the rest of them. She returned the same tight smile she offered everyone.

Pamela walked Philip and Marilyn over to a woman who

turned from her conversation with her mouth open and clutched Pamela's arm.

'Pamela, this is too much,' she said.

The woman wore pleated clothing that rose up high around her neck, and the smallest hint of diamond shone out when she tucked her hair behind her ear, but there was something ragged about her face, as if she'd come late into all this.

'What we really wanted,' said Pamela, looking around, 'was to see all our friends in one room. As a celebration.' She smiled, but her eyes were grim.

The woman shook her head.

'Denise, this is Philip and Marilyn Fetch. Marilyn and I went to school together. She's probably the person in the room I've known longest. Isn't that something?'

'Well,' said Denise. She appraised Philip and quickly moved on to Marilyn. 'You and I shall have to swap notes, Marilyn.'

'Ah,' said Marilyn.

Denise narrowed her eyes.

Pamela held Philip's arm and spoke quietly. He could feel her breath warm against his ear. 'Watch her,' she said. She pulled back and winked. 'I must . . .' She waved her hand at them and moved away.

Philip stood by Marilyn's side while she chatted to Denise. He sipped frequently at his wine and tried to look animated. The drinks girl passed by and by, topping up his glass. He turned his ear towards Denise, but still only caught every fourth word and soon lost the thread of conversation. He scanned the room for anyone he might know. His eyes roamed over the mass of talking heads.

No one, not a single recognisable person. Who were these

people that he didn't know one of them? Who was he?

Then his gaze hit on a familiar face, someone in the middle of the room whom he couldn't quite place. A father from soccer? No, too well dressed. Perhaps someone he'd done a house deal for? He looked older than Philip, so perhaps someone he'd met at Marilyn's school reunion? The man was surrounded by people. Philip looked back at Marilyn, who was still listening attentively to Denise. He took a deep breath and went in.

There were many people between him and the man, and Philip had to work hard to make his way through the crowd. He was very close when he looked up again, trying to place him—hoping a name would come. He watched the man tip his head back and laugh, an awkward, self-aware sort of laugh—and Philip knew who he was. A politician. The leader of a new right-wing party. Philip recognised him because he'd seen him on TV a hundred times. But he was too close to move away unnoticed.

The man turned to Philip, who had so obviously been headed his way. He smiled.

'Hello,' he said.

The five other men standing around him swivelled their heads to see what had drawn the leader's attention.

'Oh, hi,' said Philip. He gave a closed smile. 'I . . . sorry. I thought you were someone else.'

'Ah!' said the leader. 'I get that all the time. I was at the opening of a shop the other day and a small child asked me what a prime minister eats for breakfast.'

'Ha, ha, ha, ha,' said all the people around him.

'But did the child think you were?' Philip's voice trailed off.

54

There was a silence, then the man said, 'We can't be too far removed, can we? To be at such a gathering.' He offered his hand. 'I'm Don,' he said.

'Philip,' said Philip.

'Ah,' said the man standing right next to Don. 'Marilyn's husband?'

Philip nodded.

'I'm Hamish.' He shook Philip's hand. 'We finally meet. I can't say how Pamela feels to be back, living near Marilyn.'

Philip nodded. He had so many things that he might say, but his head had come over all cloudy.

'You're a lawyer too, aren't you, Philip?' said Hamish.

God, not that, thought Philip. 'Yes,' he said.

'Aha,' said Don. 'Let me guess—criminal or—' he waved his finger in the air '—copyright?'

'Property,' said Philip.

'You've got a little office down at the local mall, haven't you, Philip?' said Hamish.

Philip looked at Hamish, who was waving at someone across the room.

'That's right,' he said.

'Oh,' said Don.

'So, anyway . . .' Hamish turned back to the group and continued a story that seemed to be about an English defamation case involving a Tory politician and a legal student. Philip watched the other men, whose eyes were so clearly focused on Hamish and Don. He gulped his wine and noticed the cuff on his suit jacket was starting to fray. Marilyn caught his eye and raised her eyebrows at him. He summoned a small smile that told her everything was okay.

The story evidently finished, because all the men were laughing. Philip smiled and felt a murky tide wash over him, a crawling feeling that made him want to bow his head and quietly slip away. The crawling feeling was disappointment and it ran into his shoes like concrete. He looked around for Marilyn but couldn't see her. Don and Hamish were making chatter, preparing to make their excuses and turn away from him. There was an ignition in him, something akin to a flicker of anger, but he felt strangely calm. Without thought but with this strange engine driving him he said, 'I had a client the other day, a Filipino man.' He nodded at Don.

The men turned towards him.

'I'd never met him before. He just walked in off the street and introduced himself as David and asked how much it would cost for me to read over a house contract. We agreed on a price, and while I looked over the contract I noticed his surname was David and I felt a little confused, so I said to him, What's your Christian name? We had a bit of a discussion over this and he finally said, David. So I said, David David? And he said yes. Then the mortgage documents came through and you'll never guess what his middle name was.'

Don was craned towards him, chin jutting, serious in his disbelief. Hamish was looking into his glass, fingering the rim of the bowl. Philip didn't bother with the hangers-on. This was for Don and Hamish.

'No idea,' said Don. He shook his head a little.

'My children love this part of the story,' said Philip. He could feel the machine, pushing him—he was on the edge of a beautiful chasm.

'David,' he said.

56

'Ah,' Don said, and looked to Hamish whose jaw was clenched, stony.

But Philip was in swing now.

'David, David, David,' he repeated. 'And you know what?'

All the men looked at him. Did they look for his redemption or for the slaughter?

Philip turned to Don. 'I'm sorry I mistook you for someone else. I and my little office will never vote for you and your self-serving little ideas,' he said.

'Oh, well! I'm . . .' said Don.

But Philip had turned away and was moving through the crowd. He wanted to get out before the engine broke down. There was no air around him.

It was evident to the crowd that something had happened behind the man who was pushing through them. Although his head was down, he felt the weight of their collective gaze. It moved from him to where he'd come from and then back to him as though he was a strange, alien form. Philip found the nearest exit and got out.

He fell out a side entrance into a narrower hall. Philip stumbled down it as quickly as he could until he found a series of doors—a bathroom, a storage room and then, at last, a small book-lined study. He closed the door shut behind him.

His skin was clammy and he felt slightly faint; he hadn't eaten for hours. They'd skipped dinner because Marilyn had said there'd be plenty of food there. Philip hadn't made it as far as the supper table.

He slumped into a sofa and put his head in his hands. He hoped Marilyn hadn't seen what had happened. All of those people could laugh at him—the whole room could turn in their nicely cut suits and pleated frocks, their designer glasses, and laugh in chorus—but he didn't want Marilyn to have seen him.

He caught his breath, and realised that he was drunk. He'd probably had five wines while he stood there.

Then he heard her. She was singing 'Hang down your head, Tom Dooley' in her high, tuneless voice. He didn't look up.

'What do you want, Mother?' he said.

'I saw what you did in there.'

'What?'

'D-d-d- upsetting the room like that.'

He looked up. As though she could touch them, she was running her hands over the spines of the books that covered the room's walls. She was everywhere.

'I b-br-brought you up to be polite,' she said. 'Look at me when I'm talking to you.'

Philip looked up.

'You brought me up to never say what I was thinking,' he said.

She floated over to the bookshelf and waved her smoky hand over the titles.

'Same thing, sunshine.'

Why, wondered Philip, at this stage of my life do I still have a mother? Actually she was worse than his mother. Alive, his mother hadn't been quite so forthright.

'Your father was g-g-g- useful with an engine. He knew exactly where the bits went.'

She tried to pull a book out, but her hand slipped off the spine as though covered in oil.

58

'Why do you b-believe people want to know what you're thinking?' She looked at him at him briefly, without interest. 'I'm off to look at the garden.'

Why couldn't she bugger off properly? Even dead, she wasn't sensible.

He looked around the room. Snug and lined with well-made dark-stained wooden shelves. It was the sort of room Philip longed for.

In a way, his mother was right. Did anyone really want to know what anyone else was thinking? It was all about delivery in the end. Even his mother had that on her side, despite her stammer.

'Oh. There you are.' Pamela took his mother's place in the doorframe. She'd arrived as quietly as his mother had. 'What are you doing?'

'Trying to be alone,' he said.

'Is that something you do at parties?' she said. Her speech was a little slurred.

She had two glasses in her hand, one of which she held out to Philip. She'd followed him.

'A proper drink,' she said.

He took it. 'Thanks.'

The tumbler was solid and round and half-full with a whisky that seemed to contain its own amber-coloured light. She looked around as if she was surprised to find herself in this particular room.

'I don't spend enough time in here,' she said. 'We've got plans for a bigger library, closer to the bedrooms. That way at night we can just fall into bed after reading.'

Philip took a gulp of the whisky. It was complex, a brief

fire in his mouth and then the suggestion of swamps. He felt it run down into stomach and then move into his legs. He wouldn't be able to stand.

She sat down heavily beside him on the sofa and let out a long sigh.

'I'm bloody exhausted,' she said.

Her face was shiny clean—the skin of a rich woman. He looked for tell-tale signs: the tiny lines that develop where the cheek meets the ear. Marilyn worried about those lines on her own face. He felt a small sense of triumph when he found them, though they were small and barely there. This was quickly deflated by a creeping sense of his own pettiness.

She tipped her glass at him. 'Bottoms up,' she said.

Philip downed some more. He felt ruinous.

'Marilyn's wonderful, isn't she? A real coper.' She raised her eyebrows at him slightly.

What did she expect him to say? Perhaps nothing, for she continued.

'She was so popular at school. I got more boys, but Marilyn was everyone's buddy. At first I befriended her because my parents disliked her parents. But then I realised how true she was, how unpretentious.' She spoke down into her drink, swirling it in her glass. 'You don't find many people like that.' She took another sip. 'When we were young we both wanted to be teachers. Well, actually, she wanted to be a teacher and I just copied her. I didn't really want to be anything but rich.'

Philip tipped his glass at her. 'You managed that.'

She looked at him, curious. 'I don't need approval,' she said. 'Having money gets rid of that need.'

'I'm just saying,' he said. He stumbled on. That strange

fearless energy kept pushing him on. 'The only reason I'm here is because you and Marilyn were at school together and, for some reason I don't understand, you're still friends.'

'But are people so different from one another?' she said.

'I don't have a McCahon in my hallway.'

Pamela shrugged her shoulders in a lazy way. 'We're not so rich, Philip. Not the way they are on the Continent.'

She was serious and it was true, but it was a truth that belonged only to a few people.

'Why did you come back?' he said.

He'd wondered this when Pamela first made contact with Marilyn to say she was back in the country. Why now? Hamish was only mid-career at best. It was a question that hung over the whole party.

She looked down into her glass again.

'We wanted to start a family.'

'They have them,' he said, 'on the Continent.'

'You've got two lovely boys,' she said.

He nodded. The thought of them, their warm bodies curled asleep in their beds, made him long to be at home.

'Yeah,' he said. 'I'm lucky.'

'You are lucky, Philip. You're a lucky man.'

They were quiet then. The party was far away from them, a dim noise in another part of the house. After a time he waved his glass in the air. 'Is there any more of this?' he said. He would drink until Marilyn found him here.

'There's always more,' she said. Then she gave a long, tired sigh. 'It's too late for us, really, to have a baby.'

'Can't you just pay someone to have one for you?' He spoke meaning to cut her, and immediately regretted it.

61

A flash of sorrow passed through her eyes, but she quickly recovered her look of indifference.

'I'm sorry,' he said. 'That was horrible . . . I didn't mean—' He leaned his head back against the top of the sofa. He could feel his brain whirling round like a spinning top.

'Hamish has a baby,' she said. Her voice was soft. 'In London.'

He didn't look at her. It was an old story and he knew it before she told him.

'He fucked his secretary and got her pregnant. Then, because he was so distracted by his own fertility and couldn't think straight, he ruined a major decision. He blighted his career and we had to come home.'

Philip was quiet. He tried to keep hold of his spinning brain, put a hand to his forehead to steady it.

'I dream about that baby,' she said. 'I dream I'm on a boat and I'm holding it in my arms. My back is turned to the shore and I don't even bother to wave goodbye. Wouldn't an analyst have a field day with that?' She gave a little laugh.

He couldn't look at her. He could see the boat, though, and the baby.

'And now we live at the arse end of the world with a bunch of second-rate corporate lawyers for neighbours,' she said.

'I'm sorry,' he said.

'For being a lawyer?' she said.

'For being rude, earlier this evening, at your party,' he said. 'Well, I'm not sorry for being rude to him, but as your guest I should have—'

'I don't want your pity,' she said quickly. 'You might feel sorry, but it's not for that.'

They heard a door open down the hall, and a couple giggling and shushing each other. A door shut again.

'Hamish deserves everything he gets,' she said. There was a brittle note to her voice.

'Perhaps he does,' said Philip.

'But you never even gave me a chance.'

He felt shame crawl back, stickier this time. He wanted to be rid of these people and their messy lives.

The edge of a smoky blue haze reappeared in the doorway.

'Well, I can report the garden's a mess,' his mother said. She narrowed her eyes. 'Who's that little m-minx?'

'Oh, for Christ's sakes,' he said.

'What?' said Pamela.

'Oh, nothing,' he said. 'My dead mother won't leave me alone.'

'Don't be ridiculous. She c-c-can't see me,' said his mother.

'Sometimes I think I'm going crazy.'

His mother rolled her eyes.

Pamela stood up and walked to the door. She stood right where Philip's mother was leaning, as though she wasn't even there.

'Don't think you're special,' said Pamela. 'Everyone's crazy.' She gave him a small sad wave.

He raised his hand to wave back, but she'd gone, closing the door behind her.

'Well,' said his mother, eyebrows raised. 'They had a name for g-g-girls like her in my day.'

'Yes?' he said. He was weary, drunk.

'Slack.' She spat the word out. 'She—' she pointed her finger at the door '—looked just like Valerie Calvin.'

Whenever his sister was late home on a Saturday night, his mother would shake her head at breakfast the next morning and say, What do you call that hour of the night? You'll turn out just like Val Calvin.

'No,' said Philip. 'I think Valerie's probably dead. Like you.'

'Don't look so smug,' said his mother. 'You'll be laughing on the other side of your face one day.'

He had a need to shake them off—his mother and Pamela, Don and Hamish—so he stood and walked over to a small desk. It was an antique, probably rimu, with an ornate fauna and flora carvings down its legs. It probably cost thousands. He ran his finger over the smooth polished top and opened the single drawer beneath it. An expensive-looking pen sat on top of a leather-bound book. Philip tipped the pen off and took the book out. Its pages were blank.

He walked around the room examining the shelves. There were a lot of international law books, some general histories. The rest was fiction in impressive quantities and all arranged in alphabetical order. Graham Greene was present in his entirety; there were the Brontës, Dickens, Hardy, and so on, and then the expected Booker and Pulitzer winners. Philip pulled out a Greene—*Our Man in Havana*. He opened to the title page, went back to the desk and sat down. Under Greene's name, with the expensive pen heavy in his hand, he signed, Graham Greene. He put the book back on the shelf and pulled out another, *The Third Man*, and signed again. He stacked a few more in his arm and plonked them down on the desktop. He signed them all—Graham Greene, Graham Greene— each time with a bit more flourish on the final e. Once he'd been through most of the Greenes, he moved to the Ms.

Cormac McCarthy got a rough, messy treatment, Iris Murdoch a loose, cursive hand. Under Steinbeck he drew a small riderless horse. Philip signed away, with concentration and a feeling for each book. He was aware of his mother leaning on the door, watching him while she smoked some hellish imaginary cigarette. When he finished, he capped the pen and looked up at her. She nodded.

'That's a nice p-pen,' she said.

'Yup,' he said.

The whisky Pamela had given him had made him properly drunk, but somehow a space had cleared in his head. He turned the pen around in his fingers and then slid it into his pocket. He could feel its lovely weight against his hip. Then he looked back at his mother, who was humming that tune again. She looked bored, as if she too couldn't wait to leave. He took the pen out of his pocket and put it back in the drawer.

'Goodnight, Mother,' said Philip.

He walked around the wisp of her and carried on down the wide hall, back towards the hive to find his wife.

Dune Conversations

'For anxiety I would recommend you climb a hill at least once a week.'

The doctor handed over a prescription and nodded vigorously.

'Indeed, the view from the top of a hill, coupled with cardiovascular exercise, should have some effect.'

So Philip left Marilyn and the children building sandcastles in the shallows. He left behind shrieks and splashes, squabbles over shells and feathers, and he started up the large sand dune. The dunes were being regenerated after years of dirt bikes and young people cavorting in reckless ways.

People, thought Philip, are often the problem. How fine the world would be without them. Even just a little break from them would help. He imagined aliens airlifting the world's entire population for ten years and cryogenically freezing them, before returning them to the wild. They'd only bring back the good ones of course. But this, like many of his thoughts about environmentalism, didn't add up to much.

He cut up a track beside the estuary. Grasses were growing on either side and Philip remembered the head prefect at his high school. The boy had been bitten by a wolf spider while he rolled in the dunes with his girlfriend. It seemed such a sophisticated way to land in hospital, and it had left Philip with a fear of dune grasses. Whenever the children jumped in them Philip would shout, 'Stop! You'll be eaten alive!' It was this and other things that had led Marilyn to make him an appointment with his doctor.

His doctor asked all the normal questions and then asked him what was wrong. Philip looked up at the ceiling's cheap plaster tiles. He wanted to know if there were any neurobiological reasons—like, say, a brain tumour why his dead mother talked to him.

Instead he said, 'Sometimes my pulse gets a little jumpy.'

The doctor asked him if he felt anxious often. Philip wanted to tell him that there had never been a time in his life when he wasn't, but he just shook his head and said, 'A bit.' Then the doctor wrote him a prescription that said: 'Fresh air and walking.'

At the top of the dune Philip stopped to rest. Lit up before him was the sea, the great whale road. It rolled in a calm and soothing manner, denying its potential dangers. Philip thought he saw a stingray waiting in the murky shallows. He imagined a freak wave come to suck the breath from his wife and children. He stopped himself. What I need, he thought, is to be in the present more.

Behind him the estuary stretched back into a river. Paddocks full of grass and clover, happy cows and, behind them, the dark ranges. There was a small leap in him, something like joy, and Philip told himself he could be happy, if he really wanted to. There were just a few things to talk about before this could happen.

He sat and thought of conversation starters. Something like: 'James, can you invent a machine that measures the talking dead?' No. Although their friendship was founded on a love of books and blue-sky thinking, James would ask questions. 'James, I have recurring dreams where I am attacked by flying monkeys and my children hold their arms out to me but I cannot move because the monkeys have covered me in a tar-like substance that they squeezed from their nipples like black milk. Also, my mother, who is dead, comes back and talks to me sometimes.' The two of them would laugh, and James would indulge him by talking about his own dreams and Philip would feel good enough to tell Marilyn then. But this was not a conversation, this was a script. Conversations, the real ones, were unpredictable and mostly terrifically boring.

Philip dug his feet into the sand and looked out to sea. What was this gap between what happened in his head and what he could say? Marilyn said it was a pit these days, and she'd held him and she'd cried.

Squinting against the full sun, Philip could see the children rolling over and pushing each other. He saw Charlie raise a fist in self-defence against his younger brother. They'd be hungry. Marilyn was looking around, searching for him and yelling at them to stop.

He'd stroked her hair. His voice had echoed around inside him, but when he'd opened his mouth to speak all that came out was empty breath.

Love

Some days were surprising with their revelations of love, their reminders of its importance. The greengrocer came to Philip and said that he wanted a divorce. He seemed about to burst the frame of his large body.

'On what grounds?' said Philip. He searched in darkness for his name. Tony? Johnny?

'My wife's a bitch,' said the greengrocer.

Philip had never had more than a weather conversation with him prior to this. He bought fruit and veg from him most weeks, even though the prices were not competitive. The produce was good and Philip liked the guy. He wore a striped canvas apron which seemed to state a seriousness about his profession. He held tomatoes up to Philip's nose. Smell that sunshine, he'd say, and he'd place them in a brown paper bag. Yes, he was the real deal. A man who loved his work.

'You need to be a bit more specific,' said Philip, 'for divorce.'

'Why? It's the truth,' said the greengrocer.

'Yes, but we need to state reasons,' said Philip.

'Reasons like . . .' The greengrocer used his finger as a bullet-point in the air. 'She nags me and acts like I'm no good, and she spends a lot of money on crap and complains I don't earn enough. And, as it turns out after all this time, she's a proper bitch.' He stopped for a small breath. 'I should have listened to my mother.'

'Irreconcilable differences?' said Philip.

The greengrocer shook his head. 'She doesn't have a problem. It's me who's had it. I've had it up to here.' He drew a line like a knife slitting his throat.

The skin under the greengrocer's brown eyes was sunken and dry. Philip guessed it was allergies. A man with a system under deluge. Probably all those sprays on the fruit and vegetables rubbed off after a while. Philip gave a little sigh. What occupation was free of hazards?

'Does your wife have a lawyer?' he said.

The greengrocer gave a sharp shake of his head. It occurred to Philip that the wife had no idea of her husband's intentions.

'Have you spoken to her about his?' Philip said quietly.

The greengrocer sucked in his cheeks. It was the sort of expression passed on through families. He'd probably been making it since he was a child, copying his own father. He folded his thick arms over his apron and looked past Philip to the framed certificates behind him, and then around the room.

'You know,' said the greengrocer, 'this place could do with a touch of paint.'

The bland mall music was leaking through the closed door

and into the office. Early November and they were already playing Christmas songs. They were ridiculous, those songs. I've lived here my whole life, Philip thought, and it has not snowed once. Philip followed the greengrocer's gaze to a cobwebbed corner of the room. He hadn't changed anything since Lukas had died.

'Yes, you're probably right,' he said.

'You have a wife, don't you?' said the greengrocer.

'Yes,' said Philip.

'And you love her?'

'Oh!' said Philip. 'Oh, yes.'

'Do you ever see a time when you might not?' said the greengrocer.

This was the question. Philip had once told Marilyn that the reason he knew they should marry was that he could not see a time when he wouldn't want to be with her. He'd had a few girlfriends before he met her and this had never been the case with any of them. He had thought at the time that this was a great compliment. Marilyn had pointed at a print— one of those black and white Parisian photos that were big in the eighties. They'd bought it at a garage sale when they first moved in together. 'You see that picture?' she said. Philip supposed it was probably very unfashionable now. 'Do you see a time when you might not want that on the wall?' 'Oh, no,' said Philip. 'I didn't mean it like that. Not like that at all.'

'My wife,' Philip told the greengrocer, 'is one of the best things that ever happened to me.'

'Well, you're lucky,' said the greengrocer. 'That is what I used to think about my wife.'

The greengrocer was the immigrant son from a long line

of Italian grocers. His blood held knowledge of fruit and vegetables, and of the operatic. Right now he was in the middle of his own tragedy.

'For a while now I have not been able to see how I can possibly have a future with my wife,' he said.

It was an actor's line, but it was delivered with the true fatigue of grief. On hearing it, Philip felt a deep sadness. If he had been hidden away in the darkness of a theatre, perhaps he would have cried. His sadness was not for the actor before him but for humanity in its most general and confusing sense—for the way love could break for us all, so very badly. This large man in his grocer's apron who had held a tomato up for Philip to smell had spoken about the fruit as if it were a poem or a song. Now here he was imagining the end of love.

Philip gave himself a slight shake. He tried to think of the greengrocer as a potential client.

'And what about your children?' he said. 'Have you thought what you'd like to do in terms of custody?'

The greengrocer turned to him. The man's turmoil was visible, tugging at the corners of his mouth. Philip wondered if he would recover.

'My kids?' he said. He was uncertain. He hadn't thought that far.

'Yes. If you proceed with a divorce, you will need to plan for your children,' said Philip.

The greengrocer nodded. 'You see, I hadn't thought about it. I suppose . . . can we share them?' His voice was brittle.

'Yep.' Philip nodded lightly. 'The courts favour shared parental care far more than they used to. Do you and your wife share parenting duties now?'

72

The greengrocer looked back to the frames on the wall. His lips moved but he didn't speak audibly. After a few moments he looked at Philip again.

'But I can't see my way around it,' he said. 'All the softness has gone from her. We used to have plans, you know.'

Philip folded his hands together on his lap. He was the audience.

'We thought we'd do specialty tomatoes, but no one was ready for them back then. These days everyone wants their tomatoes with the whole Jesus tree attached. Back then they'd complain if the calyx was still in. I had these beautiful Tigerellas and a woman asked me why I was selling diseased tomatoes! That's what I've had to fight.' There was still an echo of determination in the way the greengrocer spoke, but he was angry too.

Philip knew the sign in the shop. It was dusty and old-looking now. In hand-lettering it stated: 'We Specialise in Heirloom Tomatoes.' He'd never seen anything other than Beefsteak and Cherry tomatoes.

The grocer turned to look out Philip's grey window.

'Times have changed.' He gave a small sigh. 'Before you know it, we'll all be dead. And what use?' He slumped down in a chair, all the puff gone out of him.

For a change, Philip found himself in Marilyn's role, cheering through the gloom and the thickening of arteries. It was not his natural role, but for now it was necessary.

'It sounds to me like you need a holiday,' said Philip. It was the only thing he could think of. A light and shallow comment, but the sign on his door did not say therapist.

'No.' The greengrocer shook his head. 'I can't afford a

holiday. It's a divorce I need,' he said.

Was it the way he said it? A demand. Or was it Philip's tentative trial with optimism? It may even have been a desire to see some rare tomatoes beneath a freshly painted sign. Whatever, Philip was at once determined that this divorce must not proceed.

This may have shown on his face, because the greengrocer said, 'Look, I'm gonna get her, she's down in the shop. Then we can move this along.'

He was out of the room before Philip could protest, leaving behind him a large empty feeling, a hole which Philip knew it was possible he might fall into. He felt all twitchy. He stood up and did a few star jumps.

Philip thought to phone Marilyn. She'd have the right phrase. But there was also this: a determination to do his work alone, to find his own way through. There was no planning for these encounters. There was no way to know how the greengrocer's wife would turn the course of events. This time Philip would fall on his resources, not his sword.

The greengrocer returned with a woman whom Philip had seen around but had never put with the greengrocer. Certainly he'd never seen her in the shop before. She was beautiful, and her casual clothes were sharply pressed. She looked around the room and gave a little sniff.

'Would you like a coffee?' said Philip. He'd read about the importance of beverages as social lubricants.

She shook her head.

'This is my lawyer,' said the grocer. 'I want a divorce.'

'What?' she said.

'You heard me,' he said.

'What lawyer?' she said.

She looked at Philip when she said it. She glanced at him as if he was just another passenger on a crowded train.

The greengrocer pointed at Philip. 'This is him, this is my lawyer and he's getting me a divorce.'

'Well, actually—' started Philip.

The greengrocer's wife cut in. 'What's going on here, Dennis?'

Ah, thought Philip. Dennis. Not a typical Italian name at all.

Dennis exhaled loudly.

'Have you been fooling around on me, Dennis?' she said.

Dennis placed his large hands on his hips.

'And when, in between running the shop and making sure we have enough money for food on our table, and looking after our kids, would I have time to make love to another woman?' he said.

His wife waved her finger. She was a beautiful finger-waggler.

'Uh, uh,' she said. 'I look after the kids. Don't tell me you look after the kids when that is my job.'

'So what are you doing when they're at school all day? And you're buying fancy curtains over the internet and chatting to your friends? While I'm serving customers and ordering alfalfa sprouts. What's internet shopping got to do with our children?' said Dennis.

'The curtains needed replacing,' she said.

She turned to Philip, to explain.

'The cat put her claws through them. They had these long narrow rips, so when you pulled them and it was still light outside the light would come right through the slits in the curtains,' she said. 'They were beautiful red velvet, like at the theatre.'

'I like light,' said Dennis.

'They made the place look a dump,' she said. 'You don't notice that stuff, but other people do. You keep everything until it falls apart.'

'I don't care about what other people notice. Everything is replaceable with you,' said Dennis.

'Just things, Dennis. I'm not the one who's doing the chucking out here,' she said.

'And if you hadn't got the cat we wouldn't have needed new curtains. You're so worried about other people? Well, I'm other people!' Dennis rubbed hard at his forehead. He looked at Philip. 'I'm allergic to cats.'

'No you're not, you just don't like them,' said his wife.

'I don't like alfalfa sprouts either but I don't sneeze every time I see one,' said Dennis.

Dennis's renewed bluster was running out of steam. This was Philip's chance to alter the tone. What was his gambit? What sharp insight would cut through the animosity? He thought of a few things. But no such knife existed. I won't even think, he told himself. I'll just trust my instincts.

'I can see you are both very upset,' said Philip. That sounded right, just a statement. 'Perhaps, it could just be—' he paused '—it might just be that, beside the curtains and the cat and the sprouts, that one of you has a kind word for the other.'

Dennis and his wife had their arms folded. They stood side by side, looking at Philip. The wife gave a little eye-roll, then turned a steely gaze on Philip.

'What are you?' she said to Philip. 'What sort of operation are you running here?' She turned to her husband. 'Dennis, what is this? What are you doing to me?'

Dennis shook his head. He looked on the verge of tears.

Philip kept trying.

'It could be that you still love your wife, Dennis. You might just need some time alone together. Children are truly wonderful, but they do make your life complicated. And with running the shop as well.' Philip paused. There was something else as well, something he should say. 'And you should know, you should both know, that I would happily pay a bit extra for heirloom tomatoes.'

Philip wasn't sure if it was going to work, but he felt it covered all the bases. Dennis and his wife stood and stared at him. There was a long stretch of silence. Philip felt his face flush a little, but he didn't try to talk. He considered that the silence, whilst uncomfortable, didn't need to filled by him. The Christmas music leaked through to the office still, urging that their days be merry and bright.

After a while Dennis spoke.

'In the face of your relentless optimism, all I feel is an urge to die sooner,' he said.

Another long silence ensued in which they could hear each other breathe. The heart, though worn, continued its good work. Philip didn't try to look at them. He was beaten. Life-coaching wasn't his thing and he should have known better than to try. After lunch he would go and talk to mall management about the Christmas music. They would, as they did every year, ignore him.

Then Dennis's wife spoke. She turned her head towards

her husband and held her face like a beautiful drunk Ingrid Bergman. It was an inspiring pose.

'What is this man talking about, Dennis? You don't love me any more? Is that what I just heard?' she said.

She was on stage too, but she meant it. Her performance was so good because it was true—she still loved him.

Dennis looked at his wife. He spoke in a voice that Philip would later describe to Marilyn as 'dolce', and Marilyn would laugh at him and say what the hell do you mean, and he would say that Dennis's voice was soft and rich like a gorgonzola but utterly sad.

Dennis said, 'We don't laugh any more.'

'No,' said his wife. 'Nothing's funny.'

And this was how Philip left them. He felt he had done his work as a human being and was not needed as a lawyer, so he stood and walked out of his own office. He put up the 'Back in 30 minutes' sign so that they would have no interruptions. He walked around the block to his favourite café, a small deli outside of the mall that was struggling in the current climate but run by people who believed that life was better with decent coffee and a small piece of good cheese.

Philip ordered a black coffee. The crema was perfect, a swirling light caramel, and while Philip sipped at it he imagined the possible tomatoes—boxes of glorious reds, yellows and purples, bastard variegations that were born of trial and error. The tomatoes were an abundance, evidence of joy. They were tomatoes raised by people who were passionate about beauty in its many guises, who loved the soil and celebrated the peculiar varieties it was capable of producing when cared for as an actor cares for the script, or a wife for her husband.

The Bookshop

The bookshop was a golden space. There was nothing particularly special about the building itself, just that the proprietor and all the people who worked there and most of the people who shopped there cared about books. In what was considered by most to be a dying world, this was something. The shop was stacked with books, wall to wall, and it was light and warm and soothing. Small handwritten notes promoted new titles. Readings were held there, with wine and olives and small salty crackers, and sometimes Philip and James would slip in and listen to novelists or poets read from their work. Yes, the bookshop was golden in Philip's consciousness. When he entered the doors he felt his bowels relax.

He was walking towards the bookshop, humming alongside a noisy inner chatter which today alternated between a rather generalised critique of growth-based economics and what meat he'd buy for dinner, when he saw James. James was looking at the lovely strong calves of a woman in front of him and thinking 'somehow a dog/has taken itself & its tail considerably away' dum de dum, a poem that he'd been trying to memorise that morning. It was morning-tea time and the crowds were swirling around them, anxious to get to their coffee. Philip pulled James out of his reverie by shouting at him.

They gave each other an awkward hug. That's the way it had always been with them.

'You're wagging?' said James.

Philip nodded.

'Shall we?' James held an arm out towards the doors of the bookshop.

They ventured in.

'You looking for anything?' said Philip.

'Art,' said James. He gave a sigh, as if he didn't believe it existed. 'Something to take my mind off our country's diminishing research funds and the general pallidity of my life right now.'

'Oh,' said Philip.

James could be like this. He was either lamenting the lack of vision in his university department and the world in general or he was splitting at the seams with a new idea. James had once told Philip that the main reason he was in the fields of fear and stress was his own neuroses. Marilyn had used the word 'manic', but Philip would never label his friend. Especially not James who dealt with such terms professionally. It flattened a person to do that, took away their light and shadow.

Philip looked around and ran his eyes over the new releases table. He breathed in the clean and newly-inked scent of the shop. He waved at Marion. She'd been helping him find new writers for years. The shop had recently been renovated, made larger. This was a good sign, like the discovery of a new species or the development of alternative energy transport.

Today, Philip was thinking of cookbooks. Something Mediterranean, good oils that Marilyn would approve of.

'Potatoes cooked in duck fat,' he said. He felt his tongue moisten at the thought of their golden crispy skins.

James, familiar with his friend's sudden declarations, looked at him briefly, then turned back to the book he'd picked up. 'You shouldn't be eating duck fat,' he said.

James was lean and wiry. In his weekends he climbed rock faces. He didn't care about food the way Philip did. It was true, Philip's middle had thickened somewhat. He knew he should ride his bike more often. But, Philip told himself, I'm tall and if there's a little extra I can carry it well. When he'd taken the neighbour's injured cat to the vet, the vet had said that the cat was slightly overweight but he didn't mind that in an older animal. Philip had taken this as general medical advice.

'How's George?' said James. He took a keen psychoanalytical interest in Philip's youngest child.

'Sneaking around, lying. The other day Marilyn nipped to the dairy across the road and saw a small child buying lollies at the counter. She said the child looked far too small to be out alone, and then she realised it was George. He'd taken her wallet too.'

James laughed.

Philip picked up a book he'd read.

'Here's a story,' he said. 'It's about a son trying to understand his father's suicide. It's really good.'

'I'm done with suicide,' said James.

'I thought in your line of work it would be of interest,' said Philip.

James shuffled some books into a neat line. 'My brother hung himself,' he said.

'What!' said Philip.

James's family were vague to Philip. When he'd first met James at university they were all about disowning where they had come from. Over the years James had sometimes mentioned a brother, some parents up north. Philip had never met them.

James spoke quietly. 'Oh, it was a few months ago. Stupid bastard.'

'What was wrong?' said Philip.

'Self-pity, mainly,' said James. 'He walked himself out into a hut in the bush and hung himself from the rafters. Father of one, ten-year-old girl.'

'He had a kid?' said Philip. 'How could he—'

'Egocentric,' said James. 'Bigoted, self-pitying.' He did not go in for sympathy.

'You never told me this,' said Philip.

'Well—' James held his hands up. 'I assume there's stuff you don't tell me, too.'

Philip had never mentioned the blue wisp of his mother to James. But then, he'd never told Marilyn either.

Philip thought of that lonely man out in the forest. Of the person who found him, of the mother telling her child that her father was dead.

'But it was your brother, months ago,' said Philip.

'We weren't close. In fact, I hadn't spoken to him for a couple of years,' said James. 'Last time was at our parents' wedding anniversary and he got drunk and started talking about the yellow peril. He lived in Ashburton.'

Philip had read statistics about that town. James's brother wasn't improving them.

'Thank God his wife is sensible. In my opinion, they're better off without him,' said James.

Philip didn't try to press him on that. With James he knew when to shut up.

A mother holding a complaining toddler moved in next to them. The toddler was hitting her and telling her off. She put him on the ground with a sharp thump and waved her finger at him. The child started to cry noisily.

'It's a pity we can't whack them, isn't it,' said James loudly.

Philip looked at him. James was in that kind of mood.

'In the meantime the third world is getting kids that young to sew up jeans and trainers for us, working them day and night and making them live in cramped compounds, and it's illegal for us to give our kids a small slap,' he said. 'The world is so unfair.'

'I don't really need your advice,' the woman said.

'Wasn't offering,' said James.

'Let's go look at the cookbooks,' said Philip. He tugged hard on James's arm, pulled him over to the cookery section.

'But did you see the way she put the kid down on the ground?' said James loudly.

'Well, it's lucky,' said Philip quietly, 'that we're such great parents.'

What was lucky, thought Philip, was that James had

Stephanie. She was full-boned woman with a loud laugh. She took no shit.

There was a shout behind them. The child had upended the woman's handbag. The harried mother was down on the floor, telling her child off and trying to pick up all her things.

'Stay there,' Philip said to James. He pointed to a chair and thrust the novel he was still holding into James's hands.

Philip went over and knelt down beside the woman.

'My kids used to do this sort of thing all the time,' he said. 'Well, they still do, to be honest.' He picked up a lipstick and a packet of wipes. 'Here you go.'

'Oh, thanks,' she said, and took them from Philip. She closed her eyes, as if praying. 'I don't know why I tried to shop with him,' she said.

Philip winked at the child, who stuck his tongue out.

'Good luck,' said Philip.

'Yes. We all need some of that,' she said.

He looked over at James, who had his head down, absorbed in reading.

Philip dallied around politics and philosophy for ten minutes or so, then wandered back over to cookbooks. He'd been meaning to get a Julia Child for some years, but she was so fashionable now and Philip didn't want to seem like he was riding on a bandwagon. He picked up an Elizabeth David instead and checked the index for duck fat. He wandered back over to James.

'So?' he said.

James looked up. His eyes were slightly red at the rim.

'I just read the suicide bit.'

'But that's near the end,' said Philip.

'Yeah, I know, but you know what I'm like with endings.' James read them first to judge if a book was any good. 'And if you tell me a book is about suicide, that's the bit I'm going to look for. Anyone would.'

Philip sighed. 'What's the verdict then?' he said.

'It's horrible. I think I'll buy it,' said James.

'Told you,' said Philip.

'I'm not buying it to understand my brother's death though. You know that, don't you?' James's voice was stern. 'I study fear and I'm not afraid of death.'

'Who said anything about being afraid?' said Philip.

'Exactly, Philip,' said James. Then he clutched Philip's forearm, more tightly than was comfortable. 'Nothing to fear at all.'

Grand Animals

He was buttering his toast when he heard the sound of the future: a dissonant wind chime. Through the gloom he saw it. It was bright orange and flashing as it moved toward the boundary that separated his house from the untamed section next door. As the machine reversed, it sounded an alarm like a clattering of spoons in his head. Such was its insistence, its proximity to the family home, that Philip felt an assault was being made on his nervous system. He was delicate. He'd woken in the night after dreaming that his children were in some nameless danger, and had lain awake unable to shake the dread off. And now this plastic orange light winked at him. It affirmed that to lay down arms was not an option. Philip gulped his coffee.

The machine rolled easily over the long grass of the vacant section and started to dig at the base of a large pohutukawa tree. The tree was one that Philip had often looked upon as a window to another time. There was something transformative about a section of wilderness. Philip remembered the long days of his own childhood, lost in the bushy wilds of the hills behind his house. The children he ran with—those boys and girls who spent their orphan days hunting moa and making futile attempts to light fires from rubbing twigs together—played out their secret lives in the wilderness. Those same hills were now covered with houses.

Philip had encouraged his own children to play in the section next door. He'd strung a rope up over a large branch of the tree to make a swing. Children from nearby houses came and joined in sometimes. He kept a loose eye on them from the window, pleased that his sons would develop a sense of independence. Philip had read an article about perceived danger. He explained this to Marilyn when she first objected to them going off alone. The study estimated you'd have to wait six thousand hours before your kids got kidnapped off the street outside your house. Marilyn said she was more worried they'd crack their heads open when the swing broke. Philip pointed out that the section gave him and Marilyn time alone without having to put the kids in front of the television. Yes, the section next door was a gift for the whole family.

Philip knew that the section was up for development, but there'd been issues with access that had allowed him to ignore the potential for loss. And now the machine with its steel arm moved through the dark and hacked away at the base of the tree so that in the half-light of a winter's morning Philip found himself standing next door in his dressing gown, thrashing his arms about like a drowning man.

The driver hung his head out of the digger's cab and tried to wave Philip away.

'Are you crazy? You could get hit!' he yelled.

'That's a protected tree!' said Philip.

'What!'

'You can't touch that tree!'

'Bloody hell, we don't need a hippy.'

'I'm a lawyer,' said Philip. 'And you can't do that to pohutukawas.'

The man turned the engine off. 'A lawyer, eh.'

Philip nodded. 'Property law.'

'Well then, Property Law, you'll understand that this is a private building site. This tree belongs to the developer who owns the section. He needs me to get rid of it because you can't build a house on a tree. And if you don't get off the section right now, you'll get hurt.'

'Is that a threat?' said Philip.

The driver held his hands up. 'Just tellin' ya. Read the sign at the entrance. Restricted personnel only. That doesn't include lawyers.' He turned the engine back on and went back to work.

Philip's mouth hung open a little while legal points leaked from his brain and dissipated into the cold noisy air. He tightened his gown around his middle and went home.

The children were sitting at the kitchen table, eating porridge.

'Daddy!' George held his arms out to him. 'Did you see the digger?'

Philip lowered himself into a chair beside George and looked at him.

'Yes, Georgie,' he said.

'Did you see its robot arm?' George made an engine noise and lifted his spoon into his mouth in jerky movements.

'My darlings. I'm sorry this day has come,' said Philip.

'You want coffee?' said Marilyn. 'Don't make this into a thing please, Philip.'

'They have to know,' said Philip.

'Know what, Daddy?'

Philip looked at Charlie. 'The tree has gone. The wilds have gone. There will be a house next door very soon,' he said.

Charlie copied his father's solemn look.

'Do you think?' said Charlie.

'Yes, son?'

'If we asked nicely we could ride on the digger?'

Throughout the week, Philip watched the change take place. The digger and its driver worked at a steady and productive rate. By late Thursday afternoon a large square piece of ground had been excavated. Where the tree had stood was a hole. Where the small hill had been there was a pit, its walls braced by heavy wooden beams.

Philip stood at the window, staring out at the dirt hole. Already he found it hard to remember the long yellowy grass. The breeze would blow its shiny pelt flat in the summer. He turned away to start scrubbing the potatoes. The children were in the living room, watching a movie.

This was the time of day Philip liked the most. He'd pour himself a beer and quietly get on with the dinner, letting thoughts swirl around in his head. He moved over to look for a peeler. It was then he noticed that he was being watched.

The driver stood leaning on a spade in the middle of the section. He was staring in through the window at Philip. It was drizzling and the light was low, but the driver's stare cut right through the damp and misted air. Philip blinked hard and looked in the drawer for the peeler. When he looked up again, the driver was still there, staring in at him. Philip tried to look over his hedge to see if there was another worker close by. He couldn't quite believe that the driver was staring at him so baldly. But there was no one else there. It was just him and the driver.

Still looking at Philip, the driver dug his spade into the dirt with one strong shove. Then he leaned back against a wooden strut, folded his arms and looked back in at Philip. Philip folded his arms too. He did not flinch, did not turn away. He stood very still and kept his gaze set straight.

For his part, Philip felt to look away would be to allow himself to be preyed upon by the man's gaze. He would not give up his place. They had both stared too long to pretend it wasn't happening, to move away to other things. It's strange, thought Philip, but I feel I've played this game before. Some ancient memory was pricked. His eyes were solely focused on the driver. The kitchen around him started to fade away. All the plates and cups, the fruit in the bowl became dim outlines of themselves. The room and the bare structure of the house dropped away until it was just him and the driver, out there in the pit of bare earth, staring at each other. No machine or profession to hide behind. Philip felt himself part of a grand animal heritage. Perhaps they'd bare teeth and piss a circle around themselves. This is what it came down to. He wasn't

90

afraid. Rather he was invigorated, ready for it.

Philip started to mouth 'wanker' to the man, a call to let the fight begin. But from behind him he heard her voice, his mother saying: *If you kids don't shut up, I'll bang your heads together.* Philip jumped. He broke the gaze, and turned to look for her.

But it was not the woman in blue. It was Marilyn standing behind him.

'Did you not hear them screaming at each other?' said Marilyn. She put her handbag down heavily on the table.

'What?' he said.

'The children, they're killing each other down there.'

'Oh, sorry.' He shook his head. 'Look at him.' He pointed out the window.

Marilyn looked past Philip out the window. 'Oh, it's Pete,' she said. She smiled and waved. 'He helped jump-start the car this morning.'

Philip looked out and saw the driver waving back at her.

'Don't wave at him! You'll just encourage him,' said Philip.

'Encourage him to what?' said Marilyn.

'To, you know, interrupt things.'

Marilyn shook her head and started putting the shopping away.

'You don't know. It might be a nice family that moves in next door. With twenty kids. And we'll never have to look after our own children again.'

'Look, he's still there. He's been staring at me for ages.'

Philip started to hold up his hand, whether to wave or give Pete the fingers he wasn't sure.

'That's because when you stand there looking out and

pointing while you talk he assumes that you're talking about him,' said Marilyn. She hit his arm lightly until he looked at her. 'Philip! Stop staring.'

'But I walked in here to get the dinner on and I looked out and he was just staring in at me,' he said. Philip leaned back against the bench, crossed his arms and looked at Marilyn. 'It was just like this.' He tried to set his eyes in a cold hard stare. 'Like he was readying for a fight.'

'Philip, you knew that the section was going to be developed.'

'It's evil.'

'It's not evil. It's a building site.'

'I'm just putting it out there.'

Marilyn sighed. 'Well then, why don't you do something about it?' she said.

'Like what?'

'I don't know. Stick some sugar in the petrol tank or something.'

'What?'

'Of the digger. It stuffs up the engine.'

'Well, that's obvious. How do you know that?'

'I dunno. From movies. Just stop obsessing. It's tedious,' she said.

'I'm not. Why can't you support me on this one? It's right next door.'

He turned back to the window. Pete was gone. He could see the end of a spade being raised into view, dirt flying off the end. Another hole was being dug.

'And anyway, I'll end up behind bars,' said Philip.

They heard a howl from the hall and George crying.

'Can you go and sort it out? I might strangle them,' said Marilyn.

Philip went to make an attempt at some fragile peace.

He never went to sleep that night; he could not rest. Whenever he closed his eyes he was back in the earth pit, waiting for the fight to begin. Philip could not turn his back on the scene.

Just after midnight he rose and poured out a cup of sugar. He closed the door quietly and walked out with the cup in his hand.

It was a reassuringly dark night. Every now and then a cloud parted and a slip of a moon appeared curved over the hill, a sly eye winking at him. Philip carefully peeled back the plastic makeshift fence and climbed over into the building site. It was a great dirt platform now. He stood where the tree had been, at the very centre of the section. There was something very tidy about the site—large wooden poles and boards held the dirt walls so that they wouldn't collapse. The dirt floor was flat and even now. Soon the diggers would be gone and the building of the house would commence. A family might move in. Perhaps even a family about which Philip would say, How lucky we are to have such great neighbours.

He walked over to the digger, its dark metal arm at rest. He stood with his foot on the traction wheel. It was an impressive little machine. The amount of work it could get done in a day belied its size. Philip ran his hand over the bonnet. How did a person get to create such a machine? The imagination was a wondrous thing. Philip remembered the book he'd loved as a child, one he'd since read to the boys about Mike Mulligan and his faithful digger, Marian.

Philip climbed up into the seat of the digger and held onto the wheel and put his hand on the stick-shift. It felt good to sit up that high, behind the controls. The things one might achieve in a day. On the back of machine like this, one could move the earth. Cities were built with these things.

As a young student, Philip had believed in the change he might affect as a lawyer. He had marched with the rest of them when the government introduced fees at university. He marched for women's rights and gay rights. He'd spent long nights in tramping huts, smoking joints with his buddies and discussing whether it was better to effect change from within the system or in underground activist groups. Philip believed that if he could understand the structure of an argument then he could understand how to sway it. He was idealistic and thought that he could put this understanding to use—good moral use. He could change the way things were done.

All that was years ago now. And now he also understood this—that up on the seat of an earthmoving machine he wielded power. And the need to dominate, to smash your opponent in the face until they bled—well that never fully disappeared, did it? Up there in the midnight hour, Philip gave in. He sat on the seat, driving his imaginary digger, changing the structure of the earth.

After a few golden minutes, he got down and ran his hand over the engine's bonnet.

'I'm sorry, Marian,' he said.

Then Philip Fetch, property lawyer, poured sugar into the engine's fuel tank. He walked carefully around the back of the digger, sweeping the soles of his shoes hard over the earth to make sure his tracks were covered. Then he went home and

94

got back into bed. He slept for six dreamless hours, and when he woke to the alarm, he felt contented. He had achieved something. He hadn't felt this way in a long time.

This sense of peace continued on through the family breakfast. He was attentive to the boys, and he kissed Marilyn three times and offered to make their school lunches while she showered.

Next door, the section was quiet. The driver was late for work. Philip was tempted to wait around to watch what happened, but he was nervous as well, and didn't think he could bear witness to his handiwork. It was a fine day, and he decided to cycle around the seafront on his way to work. The air would do him good.

Philip loved the ride around the coastline. Despite the local government's many attempts, the coastline was undeveloped. It was a wild, raw edge of land which was heavily fought over by the developers and those who wished it to remain untouched. As he approached the most southern point of the ride, Philip came across a large truck, lights flashing as it reversed a ton of dirt onto the side of the road. A young man with a yellow hard hat and a stop sign held up his hand to Philip.

'What's going on?' said Philip.

'Haven't you heard, mate?' He looked at Philip and took a drag on his smoke. 'The go-ahead's been given for the shopping complex.' The young man exhaled. The smoke hit Philip in the face.

Philip felt his peace burst. His stomach felt acidic. He thought of the digger with its engine full of sugar. He looked up at the truck, and the diggers and steamrollers parked on the side of the road waiting to do their work. There were too many.

'I thought it was up for appeal,' said Philip.

The young man shrugged and chucked his smoke down in the gutter. 'I guess they lost.' He shook his sign lightly. 'The sign says go, mate.'

Philip looked behind him. A line of cars was queued, waiting to pass around the cyclist who was holding them up in the middle of the road. He saw the driver behind him shake his head and tap his watch. Philip rode on.

Ducks

Philip mentioned the ducks to Marilyn while they ate dinner.

'I saw a family of ducks this afternoon.'

'Yeah? George, stop playing with your peas,' she said.

'They were all dead.' He paused to let the picture settle in his head. 'A mother, a father and six ducklings. On the stones by the bend in the creek.'

'Why were they dead? Did someone shoot them, Daddy?' said Charlie. He pointed his fork at George and made a firing sound. On the radio the economy was still collapsing and babies were dying from poisoned milk formula.

George gave a loud cry. 'He was shooting me!'

'Stop that, Charlie,' said Marilyn.

The news said the babies were getting tested. There were sounds of adults talking and weeping in a foreign language. Charlie kept firing at George.

'What was strange was that they looked perfect. Like they

were just resting,' said Philip.

Marilyn put her hand on Charlie's arm. 'Stop it, now!' She turned to Philip. 'They were probably resting,' she said.

'No. I touched one with a stick,' he said.

'What?'

'To test it. It felt like—' Philip watched Marilyn chase some peas around her plate then lift them to her mouth. Somehow this reassured him. 'It was like they were an installation, a mannequin family of dead ducks. It was very strange.'

'An installation at the creek? That would be good,' she said.

'How does a whole family die like that?' he said.

'Maybe some kids—' Marilyn stopped. George was looking at her.

'What did kids do?' said George.

She gave a quiet sigh. The prime minister was on the radio now. *We are building a brighter future* he was saying.

'Did some kids kill the ducks?' said George.

'No, I don't know,' said Philip.

Marilyn was shaking her head. 'God, I can't stand the radio on at dinner time!' She reached over and flicked the switch.

They sat there in the new silence, not eating.

'Many house sales coming in lately?' said Marilyn.

'A few.' Philip shrugged. 'It's quite slow.' He didn't want to think about it.

'Well, I suppose people will still need to buy and sell. Things don't stop completely because of a recession,' she said.

He couldn't stop thinking about the ducks. It was the way they all just sat there, upright wax models of birds, their glassy eyes staring as though they were somehow trying to tell him something.

Philip went to open his mouth. He must tell her.

'Hey, George,' said Marilyn. 'How come you're scratching so much?'

They all looked at George, who'd been scratching his head through most of the dinner. Marilyn stood behind him and ran her fingers through his hair.

'Oh, not again,' she said. She looked at Philip. 'Do you want to do the dishes or the nit comb?'

That night, after reading to them, Philip talked to the children about the stars and the galaxies beyond.

'The thing is, the universe is so big that we can't know what's out there. Like other life forms on other planets,' he said.

'Like aliens?' said Charlie.

'I don't like aliens,' said George.

'Maybe,' said Philip. He hugged George. The child was wary. 'Just stuff we can't see. Stuff we don't know about. Maybe a whole other world is out there somewhere, just like ours.'

'Do they have Lego?' said Charlie.

'Stay with us until we go to sleep,' said George.

Philip sat on the end of George's bed and leaned back against the wall.

After he had prodded a duck with a stick to ascertain that they were dead, he'd got down on his knees and put his hand on the mother duck's wing. It was not the sort of thing he would normally do. But they all looked so perfect and so strange.

Philip touched the duck, and then it happened.

He was filled with a sense of the beginning and the end, of everything. He felt infinite. He wasn't Philip Fetch but part of a larger organism, an overarching structure. Something was working through that dead bird, trying to tell him—what? There was no explanation.

He'd climbed back on his bike and cycled off again, perturbed. The sky darkened as he rode and the rain came quickly, pitter-pattering his helmet. He'd not worn his raincoat. Soon the road was black wet. He looked down and watched it move under his thin bike tyres. The tyres made little slick lines on the tarmac, and he tried to keep his body upright and those lines straight as if he were a performer in a circus and it was not a road that he cycled over but a tightrope.

Both boys had their blankets pulled up under their chins, their eyes wide on him. They watched their father's face the way passengers on a turbulent flight watch for subtle signs in the face of an air steward. Philip smiled and then closed his eyes, afraid he'd give something away.

The Insomniacs

He could hear them at night out on the street, calling to one another. Through the open window he could follow their nervous challenges.

'Hey!' one would call to another. 'I've seen you before.'

'It's my sixth night tonight!'

Their voices were strained, rusty metal hinges.

'You're a beginner, a baby at your mother's breast,' someone would shout back.

There was a competitiveness among them. They were runners in a never-ending marathon. They compared and complained about their aching backs and dry mouths. No one knew where the finish line was.

Philip sometimes imagined he heard them calling to him as he lay in bed, eyes clamped shut in the hope that sleep would pull him away. Their calls were taunts to him.

He wanted to join in. 'Try five years,' he might say. 'Try a lifetime.'

For that is what it felt like sometimes. He could not remember his life before insomnia grabbed his tail and twisted it. It was rare that he woke feeling rested or spent the night oblivious to the stunned forms that stalked the dark outside his window. Sometimes he envied the dead with their unbroken sleep.

He sat up at 1.03 a.m. with nothing to show for the three hours he'd been in bed. Marilyn slept on beside him. She was, he'd often thought, a talented sleeper.

Out on the street they were all there. He didn't know their names, but he recognised their voices. They stopped arguing and turned their sapped faces his way.

'Ah,' said one of them. 'You've finally joined us.'

'It's no use pretending,' said the one with the limp. 'You're with us.'

He joined the rag-tag procession to the beach. They dawdled and fought the whole way.

And once they got there they just stood at the edge of the road. They didn't know what to do next. Philip stood with them. It was a bright night and everyone could very clearly see the line of water rising and falling like a sleeper's chest.

Then someone pointed up.

'It's that! That thing. It's making us all crazy!' The man who spoke was so tired he couldn't remember the name for it. 'Look at it, staring at us.' He stumbled down onto the rocky shore until his feet touched the waterline. He could go no further.

They all looked up. It was almost full, the shape of a mouldy orange. Out here by the sea, the moon looked close enough to touch. Philip reached out to it, but everyone was going down onto the shore now, so he followed them.

'It's spying on us!' said another accusing voice.

'Yeah!'

'The government's behind this,' said someone. 'They've got cameras up there.'

'They're implanted,' said another.

'You mean embedded. These days everything's embedded,' said someone else.

Everyone started pointing at the moon and calling out to it.

'It wants to get us!'

'It's planning something, look at the evil eye on it!'

'Get it! Get it!'

Then someone from the group, refreshed by their collective indignation, picked up something like a shell or a plastic bottle top and threw it up into the sky. The object went up in the air and, when it came down, landed on someone's head.

'Hey!' said Philip, for it was his head the thing landed on. 'It got me! The moon got me.'

'You see!' said the first man. 'It's attacking us!'

'Hey!' everyone called out to moon. They started throwing shells and old bits of plates and stones and all the small salted oddments of the beach up into the night sky as far as they could. Of course, it all just came back down on them, but they did not look to blame one another; they were crazy at the moon.

The moon looked down with its all-seeing eye. It didn't blink. It just stayed there as calm as it had ever been and kept its big mouth shut.

Secret Life

'You know,' said Dennis the greengrocer, 'you're a funny guy.'

He was halfway up a ladder, rolling paint too thickly onto the wall of Philip's office.

Philip looked up at him. He didn't feel funny.

'Am I?' he said.

Dennis put the roller back in the paint tray and swished it around. He gave it a real wallow and then slapped it back on the wall. Fine droplets of paint sprayed everywhere. Already Dennis's workshirt was covered in a fine mist of Spanish white.

'Yeah. To look at you, you wouldn't know it, but after a while you get the feeling there's something else going on.' Dennis held his roller in mid-air and tapped the side of his head. Philip watched a drip form at the end of the roller. 'Like you've got a secret life or something.'

'Really?' said Philip. He picked a hair off the wet wall. 'I'm a family man, Dennis.'

'Yeah, I know that. I don't mean a woman. I mean like you invent stuff or you're secretly a poet or a painter. That kind of thing. You look ordinary, no offence, but once I got to know you I realised you're one of the most interesting guys I've met in a long time.'

'Oh, well, thanks,' he said. He pushed his brush into a messy corner. No one had bothered to strip the old wallpaper. There were years of paint layers, and the walls were sagging in places.

He kept his head down and his back turned because his dead mother was sitting on his desk in the middle of the room. She was swinging her legs. He knew this because he could hear them banging on the desk. She was probably picking at her nails as well, but he wouldn't look at her. She'd take that as encouragement.

Philip had stopped Dennis from divorcing his wife (that's what Dennis had told the entire fruit shop one day, his fat arm tight around Philip's shoulder: This man stopped me from making the biggest mistake of my life) and Dennis had been trying to repay him ever since. I want to help you now, he'd said to Philip. With what? Philip had asked. Did he look like a person in need of help? Each week a bunch of grapes or some fresh dates found their way into Philip's fruit and vege bags. Cut flowers had been left at the office.

Then, without warning, Dennis arrived on a Friday afternoon with a large can of paint. He'd started pulling the storage shelves away from the walls and laying out drop sheets. Philip had tried to tell him that really, it wasn't necessary. Dennis said it was. He'd said Philip's office was one step away from becoming a real dump. And what would old Lukas have made of that? Philip thought of the state of Lukas's house just before he died. Okay, he said.

'I bet,' said Dennis, 'you're not just a lawyer.'

Philip's mother gave a small grunt.

The idea floated on the air for a while.

'For instance, I'm a secret singer,' said Dennis.

'Fat enough for secret op-op-opera,' said Philip's mother.

'Really,' said Philip. He couldn't see how the paint would dry in time for work on Monday, not the way Dennis put it on.

'My wife thought I was having an affair at first, but I was singing. It's me and a couple of friends. We call ourselves the three and a half tenors,' said Dennis. 'Cause, strictly speaking, I'm more of a bass but I've got a wide range.'

He stood tall on his ladder and took a deep breath. Philip watched his chest enlarge like the felted bag of a bellows. Dennis let out a long, deep note—a kind of human foghorn—a note that would carry for miles through the mist to forlorn and blinded sailors.

'Gosh,' said Philip. 'That's quite impressive.'

'He's going to d-d-deafen me,' said Philip's mother. She put her hands over her ears and wafted over to Philip. 'Tell that man to be quiet, will you.'

Philip turned away from her. 'Have you had training?' he said.

'Thank you, Philip, for noticing. I've had a little. Mostly I practise at home and when I'm unpacking the delivery in the morning. It's good for the produce,' said Dennis.

'Oh, for God's sakes,' said Philip's mother.

Her face was wrinkled, screwed up from years of smoking

and bitter complaint. Philip took a deep breath and then let out a long noise that came from the tight pit of his stomach, from the acids that sometimes rose in the night and made sleeping impossible. There was nothing musical about it. Philip eyeballed the spectre in blue—his dead mother—and he howled with all his might.

When his breath ran out, he stopped.

'Told you,' said Dennis. 'You're a man of passion all right.'

His mother glared. 'B-Baby,' she said.

Philip didn't hate her, he just wanted her to go away.

'Gloria!' he said. Only he didn't say it. He sang it in a note that rose up and, like Tarzan crowing as he swings through the emerald jungle, wobbled to an end. He sang her name right into her face.

'Yes!' said Dennis. 'That's what we need. A prayer to wrap the voice around.' Dennis sang his own long extended 'Gloooorrrriiiiiaaaaa . . .' like the true bass he was. He came down off his ladder.

'And together. One, two, three . . .' said Dennis.

The two men stood side by side, their rollers and brushes in hand, brothers in arms against something, and sang, 'Glooorriiiiaaaaa!'

The woman in blue turned her back on them.

'Don't stop now, Philip!' said Dennis.

The two men sang her name over and over until it meant nothing, became just a sound. With each rising and falling note, Philip felt his chest warm and expand further. He copied Dennis, learned something from him. His mother faded away. They kept on at it long after it was polite, not just because it felt good. They let the room drop away from them as they kept on going, because they weren't just singing but calling; a pair of unbelievers, yet they were calling out for something more.

Decay

The days were calm, hanging around for winter to arrive. Philip got on his bike most mornings and rode to his office. He could see his breath in the air now; it wouldn't be long before the first frost. He loved this time of the year. The dying remnants of the summer vege garden had been pulled, some greens had been renewed by the autumn rain. And with the dark creeping forward at night it was increasingly legitimate for a person to withdraw into themselves a little.

Pushing off to ride down the valley and around the sea gave Philip some quiet in his head between home and work. The sun would be halfway up and there was a dew on the world so that everything looked fresh.

Recently, though, it had been a slog. His nose was blocked most mornings and he felt like weights had been sewn into his pockets. It was just a cold, he told Marilyn, but it was accompanied by an aching, too, that he did not tell her about:

111

a bone-deep ache that he considered might be the beginning of something bigger.

He brought his work home and tried to read over a contract that had just come in and needed to be settled immediately. Everything had to be done immediately these days. There was a growing expectation, particularly with young, professional, first-time buyers, that their business was the only business he should be attending to. And even despite the constant electronic contact they kept with him, those young men and women would also ring him at home in the evenings and ask questions they didn't expect to be invoiced for. Where did this confidence come from? He and Marilyn were never like this when they were young. These were the things Philip considered while he rode. Being on the bike brought you into the world. That was the difference between the motorist and the cyclist, he thought.

At an intersection Philip could see a white car approaching. He looked to make sure the driver had seen him. The driver was looking over his shoulder and talking—Philip recognised the distracted look as one he often wore as he drove and sorted out fights the boys routinely had in the back of the car. At the intersection the car did not come to a full stop; instead it crept forward and turned, completely ignoring Philip on his bike.

Philip pulled hard on his brakes and swerved out into the middle of the road. He missed hitting the car by a foot or two. He swore and slammed his fist down on the car boot. The car braked to a stop in the middle of the road.

In the car's rear-vision mirror, Philip saw an angry face look out at him. Then a young man got out of the car, leaving the engine running. He was wearing a backwards baseball cap

112

and a heavy brow, and he was holding a cup of coffee.

Philip, adrenaline and anger tearing through him, said, 'Learn to drive.'

'What the fuck?' said the young man.

'I said, learn to drive. You just about hit me.'

Philip could see the heads of two young children turning around in their car seats. Their eyes were large and curious, and they tilted and craned to get a better view.

'What the fuck is your problem? You blind?' said the man.

It was obvious to Philip that he should not pursue the argument and that in all likelihood he was going to get bashed. The trouble was how to stop it. He couldn't just leap off his bike. And now there was traffic pulling up behind them. Someone tooted and drove around, waving at them to move out of the way. Philip could either climb off his bike, lower it to the ground and prepare to fight, or he could ride away and risk being followed by a crazy guy. He looked back and saw a young woman driver waiting and watching with concern. A witness.

'You cyclists are a bunch of cunts,' said the young man.

'Oh. How very bloody original,' said Philip. 'You know what—'

He didn't get a chance to finish, because the young man tipped his cup and threw his coffee at Philip. At least that was the intention. What actually happened was that a gust of wind—the wind that all of the valley's inhabitants complained about; the head wind that Philip fought and rode into many days, making him curse the valley where he lived—that wind blew and the coffee flipped back in the air and fell over the young man and his car boot. Philip tried to squash a smile.

The young man swore again and wiped some coffee off his face. He got back into his car and, with a squeal of tyres, sped off. Philip thought of the two small faces in the back.

The young woman who had been watching got out of her car. A stream of traffic passed them slowly, people staring out.

'Are you okay?' said the young woman.

Philip nodded. 'Did you see that?' he said.

'Yes. I got the registration. You should make a complaint. That guy was crazy.'

'Did you see his coffee?' he said.

The woman laughed. 'Divine retribution, perhaps?' She shook her head. 'I stopped riding.' She pushed her fringe back to reveal a large scar above her eye. 'I go to the gym now.'

'Oh,' said Philip. His hands were shaking and his legs felt like they might collapse under him.

'You're a sitting duck out there,' she said.

'I hate the gym,' said Philip.

He went back to catching the bus with the other workers. Everyone wore earplugs and looked away from everyone else. Yes, thought Philip, the ties that connect us are rotting away. We are in the days of the final thread.

It didn't help that he and Marilyn seemed to talk past each other. Their mornings were a chaotic flurry of breakfast and lunch boxes, odd socks and haphazard teeth brushing. Philip worried about the boys' teeth; his own had cost thousands. His and Marilyn's conversations consisted of what they might have for dinner that night (Fish or schnitzel? Can we not always plan meals around meat? said Marilyn) and who would pick Charlie up from soccer practice. Philip remembered a

114

festival film he'd seen years before he'd had children. An Amish family of eight sat in prayer at a perfectly set table until the clock chimed six and the father nodded for them to commence breakfast. What discipline and terror! What devotion to the simplicity of life and work, to family and to God, even. The soul, the Soul—why had we done away with this idea?

Well, Philip pondered, but it took him nowhere. He was no believer. There was beauty all around him—light that sat in the hill's soft folds, the white edges of seawater that sprayed up against the rough black rocks. There was no reason for this beauty, no reason for its decay.

Philip tried to think back to when he first started to feel this way—overwhelmed by his body and the world around him—but the fog that had lowered over his life was impossible to see through. And that was the problem, thought Philip. I'm part of the decay. For a moment he imagined rogue cells in his body, dividing and growing, taking over all the good that remained. Marilyn suggested that he might referee Charlie's soccer this winter. The thought of it filled him with dread. He said yes.

The season started with a damp hiss. Philip recognised a few of the parents and children from the year before. School help, playgroups—that was all Marilyn's thing, he didn't feel a part of it. There were other fathers, mostly with jobs in the 'creative sector', who helped out. These fathers laughed with the other mothers in casual and easy-going ways. Nothing flirtatious, just comfortable, self-possessed men and women. Grown-ups, Philip supposed.

Sometimes next to these mothers and fathers he felt as if he knew nothing about his children, nothing about how to relate to the scene he found himself in. While these other parents were getting wise to the whole deal, he had somehow missed the lesson. Refereeing the soccer—well, that was a way to show Marilyn that he was moving through the world. He was a part of it.

There was a father Philip had seen at games before. He shouted loud encouragements towards his son, who was quite good for his age. Philip found it embarrassing, all that yelling over a game being played by seven-year-olds. Most of them just chased the ball. Charlie stuck in there, but he was no natural. He reminded Philip of himself as a child. Pedro, the son of the bellowing father, he was good. Pedro was the only reason the team scored.

Philip blew the whistle, called the ball out.

'Hey,' came a call across the field, 'that was in!'

Philip knew without looking that it was Pedro's dad. He pretended he hadn't heard.

The young boy who'd chased the ball out of field looked to him for guidance. Philip nodded to the child and blew his whistle.

'No fair ref!' came the voice again.

Not! Philip wanted to shout back. It's 'not' fair.

And what was with that name? Pedro? They were from the valley, not bloody Mexico. James had a theory that people gave their children unusual names to make themselves seem more interesting.

The game played on. Philip avoided eye contact with any of the parents. James had advised that. He said, Only watch the

116

game and don't get into discussion. He said, The audience get too emotionally involved and should be completely ignored. James was of the view that all team sports were ridiculous. After a few spats he had given up his role as a ref for Thomas's soccer team to loll in bed on Saturdays.

Small boys chased the white ball around the muddy grass. Charlie had wandered over to his friend in the goalpost. They were jumping up to hold and swing like monkeys from the top of the post.

Philip looked for Marilyn. She was chasing George around the periphery and talking to a friend. Philip shivered. The wind was bad today. Whose idea had this been? They should have been inside, drinking coffee while the kids watched movies.

Pedro saw a chance and ran with the ball half the length of the field down to the goal where Charlie and his friend were hanging. The two boys in the post, who seemed to be involved in some sort of competition as to who could swing the longest, were oblivious to the game heading their way. Philip watched Pedro aim the ball around Charlie's legs, but somehow he missed and the ball smacked into Charlie's feet which were hanging halfway down from the top of the post. The ball rebounded out. Philip blew his whistle.

'What's that kid doing in the goal?' Pedro's dad shouted. 'He's not the goalie.'

Philip felt his body go rigid.

'Get off the goal post, Charlie,' he said.

Charlie dropped down off the post. His lower lip jutted out.

'That's illegal. The goal would've been in if the kid wasn't hanging from his own goalpost,' said Pedro's dad.

'He can be there,' said Philip. 'They're only seven.'

He said it, but he felt uncertain. What was the procedure in such cases?

'No, he's not supposed to be there! I don't care if they're seven, how will they learn the rules if you break them all the time?' Pedro's dad looked around the field for other parental support. The other parents seemed to be taking James's advice.

'I'm the ref, I make the call,' said Philip. What he wanted to do was hand Pedro's dad his shirt and whistle.

Then Pedro's dad was beside him. 'Ref properly, and then I'll listen,' he said.

Philip felt his face flush. He turned to Pedro's dad for the first time. Never look at the audience James had said.

'Stop interfering, please,' Philip said.

And then, because there was a frustration welling in him that went beyond just Pedro's dad to all the Pedro's dads he'd ever met in his whole life, he spoke quietly so that only Pedro's dad would hear him. He said, 'Just back the fuck off.' He softened his voice even further and added, 'You cunt.'

Pedro's dad held his hands up in the air.

'Hey ho,' he said. He swivelled his head left and right to check on the other adults. 'Did anyone hear that?'

The other parents were watching with interest, but Philip had spoken too softly for them to hear exactly what he'd said.

'Did you just call me a cunt?' said Pedro's dad.

The word sounded ugly from his mouth and Philip was instantly ashamed that he'd said it first.

He shook his head. 'No,' said Philip.

Pedro's dad blinked a couple of times. 'I think you did,' he said.

'No,' said Philip. He shook his head. 'I didn't. But, you know what? If you shut up for the rest of the game—' he looked at his watch '—which is only ten minutes, then I will give your son the goal plus one for the inconvenience and I will also agree never to referee again, ever.'

Pedro's dad folded his arms. He nodded slowly. 'It's a deal.' He looked away from Philip and did a little snort. 'Fuck-knuckle.'

Philip held his whistle up. 'That,' he said, 'is not a word.'

He blew the whistle.

Small boys chased the ball again. Philip looked over to Marilyn, who was standing very still on the other side of the field. She had George in her arms. Even in her puffy winter jacket she looked thin, and George was snuggled into her hard so that Philip knew he was cold. She wasn't looking at him but off to the distance, to where some very dark rain clouds were rolling in. The weekend-long southerly they'd been promised was arriving. The two of them huddled there—his wife and son and, more specifically, the faraway look on his wife's face—made him want to weep.

That afternoon the weather really arrived. Philip was downstairs trying to get the gas heater going, and it just wouldn't start. The boys stood closely by and talked at him. They wanted a movie, they wanted popcorn, they were cold and wanted the heater on. Since they'd brought the house, the heater had been unreliable. It was something they were going to get fixed but never got around to. Philip put the movie on and came back upstairs to get an oil heater to take down to the boys.

Marilyn was lying on the sofa. She looked pale, and averted her eyes from him.

He stopped. 'You okay?' he said. She hadn't said she felt ill.

For a while she was quiet. The rain hit the window behind her—drops like small icy stones.

'Not really. No, Philip,' she said.

A tremor ran though him. She was going to tell him exactly what it was she felt, he knew that. She was going to tell him the thing that perhaps he'd always feared, that he wasn't good enough for her.

A strange thought entered his head—that his skin was the land's surface and his muscles beneath the skin were tectonic plates shifting and butting against each other. He looked down at his hand, which was shaking. Like a piece of seemingly stable earth, he was liable to crack at any time, no predicting when.

He wouldn't give her a chance to say it. He would get in first.

'I can change,' he said.

He spoke softly, but she heard him.

There was a whiff of a blue shadow moving at the edge of the room. A shadow in the corner like the ghost of Merlin. But what magic was his mother? Was she waiting around to watch him fail or succeed? Out damn spot was what he wanted to call. He'd always had a sense of the dramatic. But even that was fading in him. It could be, he thought, that I am seeing things. That is not my hand shaking. That is not my dead mother lingering, bluish in the corners of the room.

'What do you mean?' said Marilyn.

Philip regretted his outburst. But he kept going. He couldn't turn back.

'I mean, I can change if it helps you fall in love with me again,' he said.

He was down on his knees beside her then.

'Oh, Philip,' she said in a very small voice.

All the objects in the room seemed to move away to the edges of his vision. He was aware of every sound in the room, the refrigerator's hum, the heat pump clicking back on, the rain outside. Even Marilyn, who was not an object but his wife, even she had moved away to the edges, although he was deeply aware of her breathing, that it was faster now because there was all this time they'd spent together and their children downstairs and the misunderstandings between them that had started out small but like a rot had spread until they were two people who had once known each other very well, and now, it would seem, not well at all.

There was no blue at the room's edges. Philip didn't look directly, but he knew it wasn't there, perhaps it was never was. It was just something he'd made up.

Heart

On a morning when the cloud damped down the edges of light so that the sun seemed to have been replaced by a weaker star, Philip moped in bed. He should have been up half an hour ago because he had to get Charlie to swimming class and Marilyn was taking George to gym, but he was unable to move. A giant hand was holding him there, keeping his body on the mattress with its giant force.

'I hate gravity,' Charlie had complained when Philip made him walk over the hill.

'Why?' asked Philip.

'Because it wants me down on the ground,' said Charlie.

Philip understood this. Why did they have to live down here, plodding foot after foot? Philip hadn't had dreams of flying since he was a boy, but he could remember them. Right now, he was as far away from flying as he'd ever been.

There came a yelp from the boys' bedroom, followed by

shouting and crying. Philip would have to be the one to deal with it. Marilyn had turned the radio up in the kitchen—a sign that he should be doing something. He could not avoid his life any longer this morning: the fights over Lego blocks and accusations of violence. There would be violence, even though both boys would strenuously deny it. All Philip could do was pull the bedroom door shut on the yelping and let them go at it until a lord of flies was crowned. Which wasn't really parenting. But he was being held down by gravity's strong arm, so he had an excuse.

Somehow he managed to limp into clothes and pack Charlie's swimming bag. He would buy Charlie a snack at the pool, which went against his and Marilyn's recent agreement to spend less on coffees (a saving of three thousand dollars per annum, Marilyn estimated) so that they might go as a family to visit Philip's sister in London. The mere thought of which exhausted Philip. He got Charlie ready to leave with the barest of interactions. Marilyn was busy stacking the dishwasher. He hesitated at the door.

'See you at eleven?' he said.

They always met for morning tea at a local café after sports were finished. The boys got treats while Philip and Marilyn finished the weekend paper.

She nodded but did not turn around.

'Sure,' she said.

They would save money in the week, not on Saturdays. Neither of them could lose the Saturday coffee. Not today, at least.

Philip tried to avoid conversation with Charlie in the car

by turning up the radio. It worked for a minute or two, but Charlie's head was brimming. Marilyn said she could sometimes hear his thoughts humming.

'Daddy, did you know?'

'What?'

'Justin Bieber's my cousin.'

'Really?'

Philip had heard the name but didn't know the face. His children were moving into that world already. He had no idea who peopled it now, what sort of company his children might be keeping. And there were these low-level lies that Charlie was starting to tell. After they'd watched a History Channel show on Nazi secrets of the pyramids, he'd overheard Charlie say to a friend that his grandfather had shot a Nazi with a pistol. Charlie's friend had looked nonplussed. Philip doubted that either of them knew what Charlie was talking about. Marilyn thought it mildly amusing, but it disturbed Philip. The child lied with ease. Perhaps he truly believed the tales he told himself. Charlie's world was a compound of fantasy and fact, and he joyfully moved between the two without discrimination.

'Yes. I want to see that movie with him in it,' said Charlie.

'Mmm.'

'Dad? I want to see that movie. We could go together.'

'Um. I dunno, Charlie.'

Philip didn't want him to watch films about teenagers, not yet.

'Ohhhh! It's not fair. He wants me to see it.'

'Who?'

'Justin! My cousin.'

'No.' Philip shook his head. 'A film company wants you to see it. They pay millions for you to think that.'

'You don't even know, Dad.'

That's true, thought Philip. There are many, many things I don't know.

'Charlie, why do you say that Justin Bieber is your cousin?'

Philip looked in the rear-vision mirror. Charlie was gazing out the window, humming a tune.

'Stop kicking the back of my seat, Charlie.'

He waited.

'Charlie!'

'I wasn't kicking. I was counting the beat.'

Charlie told everyone that he was going to be a drummer. He tapped the table constantly with his fingers at dinner. Recently the teacher had told Philip and Marilyn that she was worried about his reading. Were either of them diagnosed dyslexic? she said. It often ran in families.

Philip had been silent, but Marilyn nodded. Had she already suspected this of their child but not said anything to him? What other thoughts were going on in his wife's head that he had no idea about, and where was he anyway that he did not even notice his son was having trouble with reading?

Like Charlie, Philip lived in his own parallel universe. They might be years like this: Marilyn busy with her community groups, the children and her friends, stopping only sometimes to notice the slow leak in their marriage. And Philip would go on, completely unaware of the confusion of language around him, sometimes risking the danger of the road to ride his bicycle to work. He was out there on the road, an invisible rider. In his universe, there was love, but he wasn't conscious of it, just as the motorists weren't conscious of the riders on the road. Like Philip and Charlie, their heads were awash with words, looping over and flying off in ways that made them unintelligible—senseless words bouncing around to the relentless tune of a Justin Bieber song.

Philip yearned for his wife to hold and touch him, and for him to be quiet and still and once again notice the light on the shiny leaves outside his window as a fragment of a brilliant thing. Although the world was slowly dissolving in its own cruel muck, he wanted to feel that everything would be okay. It would all be okay.

Now came the grip around him once more. The giant that was hugging him to death. He could not apologise to Marilyn again; he could not become the pathetic, sorrowful human being he had been a few weeks ago, kneeling down before her and crying. It was not fair to her. He was getting the flu anyway. He felt sweaty, and when he looked in the rear-vision mirror he saw Charlie, nodding in time to some song Philip couldn't hear, and he also noticed how bad his own colour was. Sorrow was shaping his face. It will kill me, thought Philip.

'Daddy!' screamed Charlie.

Only Charlie had seen the cyclist in front of their car. Philip had turned right and suddenly she was there in front of him. She seemed to have come from nowhere. He stamped his foot down hard on the brake and the car squealed to a stop, just missing her. The woman on the bike gave him the fingers, and he nodded and mouthed 'Sorry' to her. He pulled the car over to get out and apologise. He could hear his heart thumping in his ears.

The woman saw him pull up, and she yelled at him through the window, shaking her head. Philip felt completely ashamed. He was just like the rest of them. He put his hand on the door to open it, but the cyclist rode off again. Philip wanted to stop her and say, I'm sorry, I'm not really a motorist, I'm one of you. He felt like he might faint. His arm was too weak to open the heavy door, and perhaps he tried to push, but nothing budged. The cyclist rounded a corner and was gone.

'Oh, Jesus,' he said. He could hear his pulse in his ear, still pounding violently.

'We didn't hit that cyclist did we, Dad?' said Charlie. 'You didn't kill that lady on the bike?'

'No, Charlie. No.' Philip could barely get the words out he was so breathless. 'I think you probably saved her.'

He looked at Charlie in the rear-vision mirror and gave him a weak smile. The child looked back at him, serious, concerned and slightly triumphant at having saved a life.

'Yeah, I saved her, Daddy,' said Charlie. 'Lucky for me, eh.'

Philip wanted to cry. He put his head down and tried to take a few deep breaths. Something stopped him—the air around him was too tight.

'Dad, you look funny,' said Charlie.

'Yeah, I think I'm getting sick.'

'Are you going to puke?'

Philip considered it a possibility, but he shook his head weakly.

Charlie hummed a little.

'When can I stop going to swimming?' said Charlie.

'When you can swim,' said Philip.

They had this conversation every week. Philip didn't have

enough energy for a round of questions and answers today.

'But, when *will I* swim?'

'I don't know.'

'I'm a really, really good swimmer.'

Philip nodded.

'But when will I stop going to swimming?'

'Charlie!' Philip raised his voice as much as he could with the giant hugging him. 'Please, stop talking. I will buy you anything you like at the café if you don't talk for the rest of the car trip.'

It was mean and the worst type of parenting, Philip knew that. Charlie knew it too, but he also knew a good deal when he heard one and kept quiet.

Somehow Philip got the car to the pool. Charlie stayed silent all the way, and Philip was grateful for that.

Charlie's lesson started and Philip leaned heavily on the railing watching him. He was actually quite good in the water, like his mother. He might not read, but he could kick. His long, skinny body was propelled through the water by strong kicks. Big feet, the instructor had told Philip a few weeks ago. It helps. He was still learning to breathe properly, and his arm movements were jerky and awkward, but look at the little bugger go!

Then the giant, who had really only been teasing Philip all morning, decided to pick him up and throw him down—although Philip didn't so much fall as collapse. The giant chucked his toy, and Philip fell with an absolute fear that held a deep and certain knowledge that it was possible to lose everything. There was a crippling feeling in his chest, and he clenched his hand to the place where his heart was, as if to make a final attempt at protecting it.

He landed on the hard wet linoleum with its small round bumps that stop children from slipping and hurting themselves. Philip's long malfunctioning body fell in the puddles, his jeans and tee-shirt soaking up what they could. Those small discomforts went unnoticed by him. There was a vice around his chest and it was almost a relief to lie on the hard floor. He had the realisation that this was where he'd been headed for a while. And then he wanted to go with it, to give up a little.

Time stretched out its long arms. He heard children squealing and splashing in the pool and he heard the water— he heard each droplet fall and repool. He saw the blue filtered light that filled the room, and he saw the way it reflected up onto the domed ceiling so that its flickering looked like shoals of fish swimming above his head. His thoughts were a fish's iridescent tail that darted this way and that, one moment shimmering, the next gone into the deep.

He tried to take a gulp of air. The pain increased. Then there were people—some faces above him. Their voices came to him from far away, as if calling long distance on some ancient connection. He tried to look for Charlie and perhaps he heard him calling out Daddy, Daddy! but there was that giant hugging him around his chest again, hugging him to death, and there was a strong sense of wanting to drop away from it all down to the bottom of the ocean, to be taken out of pain.

He drifted on the floor to nowhere in particular, nowhere he could name, and then he did hear Charlie's voice and he came back again. Someone was standing over him, looking serious. This person spoke with a quiet authority, asking Philip his name and the name of the prime minister. Philip wished he had the energy to say, But he's no one I would have voted for, but the person asked him what he felt, what was wrong with him? Philip wanted to say that aside from everything else, what was really wrong was that he'd been a fool. In his head he had a picture of light on leaves, but he couldn't make the picture turn into words he might speak. I do not want to be alone, he might have said if he could. Do not let me be alone.

What happened after that, he did not know. He was not a participant in the world.

In the cardiac ward of the hospital, the surgeon told Marilyn that Philip's heart attack was a big one and that they were surprised he'd survived it. The surgeon called Philip a fighter. He said that word a couple of times, and each time Marilyn heard it she searched the surgeon's face for evidence that he was lying. They were probably trained to use certain terms. Were there any signs? said the surgeon. Did she know that he was unwell?

'One of the big symptoms is denial,' said the surgeon.

Marilyn knew that. She'd learned about denial in a first-aid course.

In the operating theatre, Philip's chest was opened up for the surgeon to observe his heart. The surgeon touched the battered tissue with his gloved finger and marvelled yet again at the damage a body could endure. He was a man who loved his job—how many hearts had he operated on now? He'd lost count. But still there was a feeling he got when he opened up a chest and saw the thing for the first time, beating away. He sometimes got that feeling listening to Ligeti. He couldn't say what it was, but it mystified him and lightened him at the same time. He shook his head and got on with his job.

Philip slept through it all. He was sometimes in the dark completely and other times he found himself out in the world, standing in a paddock in the countryside. Above him the moon was full, a tin disc in the sky. Thin webs of cloud were dotted around, but most of the stars were visible. What brilliant points of light! Under that full moon, shiny blades of grass were turned to silver-white so that if he blinked he saw the paddock transformed into a large flat glacier.

Philip walked out into the white world, breathing deeply. The air smelt of snow, of rain on grass. This was possibility, sweetness! To be lifted out of the body by light.

Then the perspective changed and he was soaring above it all, looking down, like a hawk circling and being lifted up on currents of air. The moon was in the hawk's eye. The silver grass whispered to him. He was in the world and the world was in him. Philip breathed it in. He held his arms as wide as he could. And he sneezed and sneezed and sneezed.

The room he woke up in was artificially darkened, curtains drawn and lights down low. He saw the metal railing around him, the cheap plastic jug and cup on the table. He shut his eyes and went back to the glacier. For a while he wandered back and forth between the room, dull and devastatingly real, and the ice, a bright dream landscape.

A beeping sound invaded the white world and Philip

searched for the hawk, but no, it was not a hawk—it was an alarm, a sound as jarring to sleep as a sneeze—and he woke again. The sound came from a machine he couldn't see because he was held down in the bed by tubes and pins, and by the pain of the cut in his chest. He thought of trees felled—no, not felled, but diseased and inwardly collapsed so that they didn't fall but simply shrank back into the ground.

In the room he could hear her. A soft whistle on the out breath. Marilyn. She was over in a corner, asleep in an armchair. Her hair was not brushed and it fell across one cheek. Between her brows was a tight line. He wanted to go over and crouch beside her, push back her hair and smooth the line out of her face, but that was impossible. He wanted to tell her about the paddock, the glacier and the hawk.

When he closed his eyes he could see it all again; he could bathe in the silver and the white. The machine that monitored his pulse let out a beep every time his heart beat, a reminder that it was working. Other than that, the room was quiet.

Hunting Reverie

Desire is a fog that in the early morning lies over the valley and houses. It leaks through the gaps in the floorboards and covers the dark furniture of the house and its sleeping inhabitants like a soft blanket.

And so it was that when he opened his eyes Philip noticed that the light had changed. It was not the sharp, clear light of a valley morning; this morning's light was muted and blue around the edges, as if the entire house had been raised up out of its crevice and pulled into the mountains. He woke Marilyn with a shake.

'We're here,' he said, 'we're really here.'

'Put the coffee on,' she said, 'and don't forget your gun this time.'

Serge was waiting for him in the little street behind the house. They brushed each other's cheeks and got into the car.

'Tonight we shall dine like kings,' said Serge. He laughed and lit a cigarette.

They set off out of the village and into the countryside. Every field was row after row of grape vines so that the hills looked like a head of neatly braided hair. It was harvest time, and they passed a number of workers and noisy machines that rode over the top of each vine, cutting the grapes as they went.

Serge tooted and waved out the window. Sometimes he slowed and called out to one of the workers. He raced his car down the narrow lanes and around corners, swapping sides of the road so often that Philip could not remember which side they should be on. Twice they got stuck behind large lumbering trucks laden with grapes. Grape juice ran out the corners of their containers as the trucks bumped over holes in the road. Serge hunched over the steering wheel and grumbled. Then, without heed, he pulled out around one of the trucks and sped past it, one side of the car almost running into the ditch. Philip felt a rush of panic and clutched at the edge of his seat. Serge was very relaxed about it and continued to check the vines to see if he recognised anyone out there as he overtook.

At one field Serge stopped the car and called out to a man who was leaning against a truck. The man had large stained hands that he wiped a few times on his overalls before he kissed Serge's cheeks. They had a loud, unintelligible conversation and Serge nodded a lot. The man handed him something, and Serge slapped him on the back and hugged him. Serge came back into the car. In his hand he held a cassette tape.

'Listen to this,' he said.

The song was in English, but it was not one Philip recognised. The verse, a lament for tragic lovers, rose into a chorus of murder and grief with banjo and fiddle.

'I weep at this song.' Serge wiped his shirtsleeve across his face and sniffed. He looked at Philip and clasped his upper arm. 'Do you hear it, Philip? It contains the world.'

They drove for a few more minutes, Serge sniffing and singing quietly to himself. Philip watched the countryside. Animals seemed not to exist in this world. Not once did he spot a cow or a horse, not even a single sheep. It was a lonely scene. Philip felt his ancestors line up, a row of men on horseback with dogs at their sides. They were all shaking their heads.

The car dipped down into a little valley. Through some trees Philip spied a lake, and a fish jumping.

'Hah!' he said, and pointed at it—a real live creature. 'Fish.'

Serge shook his head. 'It is ruined. They have piranhas in there now.'

He pulled the car into a small siding beside a thinly wooded field and turned to Philip.

'Now, we must focus like the animal,' Serge said. He poured a black coffee for Philip from his silver flask. 'We must embrace our true selves. Forget for a moment our wives and children, our broken pumps and land taxes.' Serge downed his coffee and put his gun on his shoulder. 'Let us commune with nature.'

Though small, Serge had the wiry legs of a sprinter. He was a plumber who declared that he never got sick because his body was used to dealing with shit.

They walked into the wood. Philip's gun was awkward

136

at his side. He kept checking the safety, worried that he'd accidentally shoot his foot. He followed Serge until they came to a clearing. Through a series of complicated hand gestures he understood that Serge wanted him to wait by a tree. He did as he was told. He leaned against the rough bark of a large tree and looked around.

The air was starting to hum with crickets and he could see waves of heat. The day would be a scorcher. Philip thought about diving into the lake, and then he remembered the piranhas and a horror film he'd seen as a child where a grown man was stripped to the bone by a school of fanged fish. A dragonfly hovered in front of him. It was a beautiful insect, a flying jewel. How the children would love this. He pictured them, butterfly nets and fishing rods in hand, acting out their true wild natures.

Serge tapped Philip on the arm and pointed. Between two poplars, a lone grey rabbit sat sniffing the air. It was a plump rabbit, enough to feed a family of four, once they had worked their way around its delicate bones.

Perhaps aware of the hunters but hungry enough to take a risk, the rabbit began to nibble at the brown grass. It concentrated on one area, then took a few hops and started on another. The clearing in the woods had enough trees close by for a rabbit to run for cover. In autumn, Serge had told Philip, he came near here to collect mushrooms. Serge was hazy on exactly where. Such information was never openly shared.

As it moved, Philip regarded the rabbit from a few angles. Yes, it was a rabbit living off the fat of the land. With its ripe body and soft white fur it was a celebration rabbit—Marilyn might even be convinced to make dumplings. It hopped and nibbled at the sparse green undergrowth. Philip could almost smell the rich stew of wine and lardons and the sauce he would mop up with his crusty bread. Perhaps he licked his lips too audibly, because the rabbit startled and ran. Serge fired a shot, but the rabbit was gone. Serge swore.

'That was a good one,' said Philip.

Serge waved his hand. 'Ah, it's no problem. There are more rabbits. But we must focus, Philip. Like the animal, remember.' Serge pointed two fingers at his eyes and then back at the field.

Philip nodded. He attempted to immerse himself in the countryside. Now that it was late summer, the sun had scorched the tall grasses to a golden brown. The soil was dry and the roads and houses by the fields were covered in a fine layer of dust. The place looked trodden over and done in. Philip could feel the earth pulse with the rising heat. He yawned. Serge shushed him.

'Sorry,' whispered Philip.

'Like the animal,' Serge mouthed back at him.

Philip leaned his head back against the tree. He closed his eyes and tried to think like an animal. It was difficult. Because of his allergies he hadn't had pets as a child. The boys had begged for a cat, and they had one for a while, but they had to return it because it insisted on sleeping on Philip's side of the bed and he came out in a rash. I am an animal, he told himself. I am only separated from the rabbit in the field by a few removes. Take away my knife and fork, take away my gun and coffee, what am I? These thoughts stimulated Philip into opening his eyes. The sun had risen further in the sky and he was momentarily blinded by the whiteness of the day. He shielded his eyes and looked to the clearing. The celebration rabbit was back. Stupid, thought Philip. Had it not seen the gun? Why didn't it question the men? Then it occurred to Philip that the rabbit was just a bit too clean, a bit too well fed. He looked at Serge, who had his rifle on his shoulder and had closed the bolt. The rabbit was within his sights.

'No!' Philip heard his voice ring out in the field. The rabbit ran. Serge's shot hit a tree. He swore again and shook his head.

Philip had imagined the scene of himself arriving home with slightly bloodied trousers, his gun slung over one shoulder and a rabbit over the other. This faded away. Perhaps he was destined for vegetarianism.

'Sorry,' he said. 'But I do believe that rabbit belongs to Henri, Luc's son.' He gave a nod, certain now that the creature was indeed little Henri's birthday rabbit.

Serge stared at him, his large sunburned nose wrinkling slightly with incomprehension.

Serge dropped Philip outside the gate. Philip waited for Serge's car to pull away before he removed a rabbit from its supermarket packaging. The flesh was cold from the refrigerator, so he gave it a quick rub with his hand and held it by the legs and spun it in the hot sun. By the time he'd chopped it up, Marilyn wouldn't notice. He arranged the rabbit on his shoulder.

The boys heard the gate open.

'Daddy, Daddy,' they called out, and ran over to him. 'You caught a rabbit! Was it a fast one? Can I see its tail? Its eyes look funny.'

Philip let them inspect the rabbit as he placed it on the chopping block outside.

'Where's its fur?' said Charlie.

'Serge is going to make a little rug from it,' said Philip.

'I want a rabbit rug!' said George.

'Me too!' said Charlie.

They all stared at the dead lump of animal, its neck stretched back awkwardly on the block. Serge had thought it odd when he'd asked for one without a head. That was not the way it was done.

'Now, stand back, boys. Daddy is going to get the rabbit ready for Mummy.'

Philip raised his cleaver and chopped it into the rabbit's neck. It took a few blows to completely sever the head, and with each blow Philip felt a little wave of nausea.

'Ewwww,' said George. 'I don't like this rabbit.'

'Well, it's much better once it's cooked, George,' said Philip. 'Just like roast chicken.'

That night Marilyn served the rabbit with dumplings in honour of her husband the hunter. She placed the pot on the table with a sense of ceremony that Philip could not quite meet. The boys had separated the image of rabbit on the chopping block from the delicious meal on their plates, and they ate with the appetites of growing children and talked of guns and rabbit rugs. Philip, who found himself without appetite, just picked at his dumplings and went to bed early, complaining of a stomach ache.

Titan Arum

After facing death in all its sharp-eyed, feathered glory, Philip had an urge to explore the quiet edges of the world. He took his bike out and travelled on his own steam. He rode through the spring headwinds and pollens with their orange dusts. He rode up hilltops and down rivers, along narrow vertiginous tracks. He took the pebbled shoreline paths out to distant rocks on which seals reared their pups, and then he rode home again, into the loving arms of his wife, the messy comfort of the family living room. Summer came, and he felt fit and strong and he invited James to come out with him.

On the way back from a long ride, Philip tried to explain himself to James. He said it was as if his old blood had been changed in a cosmic transfusion, and now his new blood ran faster in his veins. And he said. 'I've got this need in me to, you know, really push myself beyond—'

'Yeah, yeah,' said James, who was sweating beside him on

his own two wheels, 'your symptoms are typical of someone who's narrowly avoided death. Why it took you a heart attack to work out you needed to exercise more strikes me as completely illogical, but there you go, you're nothing new.'

He gave Philip a whack on the back as he sped past him.

'It's not just exercise,' Philip shouted out after him. He was breathing hard now, but he kept on talking all the same, for he was a man who'd almost lost the ability. 'It's a desire to go beyond where most people go and to get there myself. I want to push the boundaries of the outer suburbs, kind of like a pioneer . . .'

Then he had to shut up, because he was almost winded from effort. He kept a steady pace though. It felt good to push his working heart as hard as it would go. He looked past James's sweaty back to the sky, blue and cloudless, and that's what he imagined he was riding into, endless sky, and it kept him going. Then they were back on the outskirts of the valley's hilltop houses. They pulled off the end of the gravel road, and walked to the top of a small rise and sat down.

There was a faded sale sign banged into the ground below them: 'Create you're own rural retreat,' the sign said. James snorted at the misplaced apostrophe. He pointed at a small run-down house that was near the boundary of the section.

'Do they think we're idiots?' said James.

They sat at the top of the rise, drinking from their bottles and letting the breeze stream over them. It was heading towards summer and the sun was getting higher in the sky.

The sun was the same hot ball of gas and fire that it had ever been, and yet looking at it caused Philip to marvel at the lucky collusion of circumstance which had brought about its existence. He did that a lot these days. It was like he'd been storing up all that wonder for years, and now it was coming out like some dormant flower that had finally reached the right conditions to bloom.

'James,' he said because he was feeling invigorated by the ride and by the very fact of life, 'what do you make of the idea of ghosts?'

James swirled some water in his mouth, then spat it out on the ground beside him. He squinted back at his friend. 'Spectres?' he said. 'Phantoms?'

'Yeah,' said Philip.

'Maybe some sort of cross-wiring in the sensory maps.' James tapped the side of his head. 'It's interesting. But I met a guy recently who tracks ghosts for a living. Makes a modest amount off it too.'

'Really? And does he believe in them? I mean does he really believe he's tracking ghosts?' said Philip.

'Seemed to.' James shrugged.

'My dead mother talks to me,' said Philip.

There it was out in the open, like carrion for picking. James didn't look at him, but past him to the wide sky. Philip thought perhaps he needed to fill in this space with more information.

'She wears a blue suit and she comes and goes as she pleases.' He gathered more examples in his head, as if she were a thesis to prove. 'And last night I was cutting up the carrots for dinner and she asked me why I did sticks, not rounds, because everyone knows there's more nutrition in a round when it's cooked. And she smokes. Menthol.'

'Rounds?' said James. 'Was she that annoying alive?' He

squinted at his friend. His crazy friend. 'You can smell the cigarettes?'

'Yep. Pall Mall. Same as always.'

'The thing is, Philip.' James was trying to split a blade of grass to make a whistle. 'The fact of it is, we're all going to die. You might die sooner than me, or maybe not.'

'Just because I've had a heart attack doesn't mean I'll die before you. You might have cancer cells in you right now that you don't even know about,' said Philip.

'A cheering thought,' said James.

'And you don't think I know this?' said Philip. 'You think I'm imagining conversations with my dead mother because I'm scared of dying?'

James looked away from him. Sometimes Philip thought that for a person so heavily invested in the positive possibilities of scientific discovery, James could be a little gloomier on ideas like the future than he should be. He of all people should know that it wasn't fear that kept a person alive, it was curiosity.

'So you see your mother?' said James. 'Every day?'

'No,' said Philip, somewhat deflated now. 'Just from time to time.'

'Interesting.' James looked at Philip thoughtfully.

'Now you're going to say I'm crazy,' said Philip.

'Yes, but—' James waved his hand dismissively '—what's interesting is that I've had this idea after talking to that guy who tracks ghosts. You see he's got this device that allows him to pick up low-frequency signals and I wondered . . .'

While James explained an idea for recording the sound of Philip's dead mother, Philip gazed up at the sky. He let James's

144

talk of infrasonic research wash over him. He had no desire to capture his mother's voice. He'd heard enough of it. No, what he felt above all was relief. He had finally told someone. And now he would ride home and tell Marilyn this evening. She would call him a fool, or not. They'd had some good talks while he convalesced. It was incredible to him how misplaced some of his thoughts were—how wrong he'd been about so many things he assumed she thought of him.

'So,' said James, 'what do you think?'

'Maybe,' said Philip.

There was an image in his head of his mother, alive and working in her garden. She was moving some of her bright orange calendulas around. She had been an advocate for companion planting long before it was popular. Philip had brought the mail in to her. Her face was hidden beneath the large sunhat she always wore in the garden, and she dug furiously while he stood there and argued with her about a parking fine she refused to pay. Stop treating me like a child, she'd shouted. And he'd left her feeling as if he had a small piece of gravel in his shoe that he couldn't remove and had to walk on for ever more. That was what talking with his mother felt like most of the time, and he had never figured out a way for it to not be like that. And the next time he saw her she was dead. Which was how things go, plain old living and dying.

James pulled a reefer and a lighter out of his chest pocket and waved them at Philip.

'Want some?' he said.

'Is that bad for my heart? You know, I don't even drink much now,' said Philip.

'I don't know,' said James. 'I'm more about the head. I do

believe, without having done the definitive research, that taken in occasional doses a bit of pot is actually quite good for a person.'

So they sat there passing the smoke back and forth, and Philip felt a pleasant sunny-day feeling wash over him, similar to a feeling he'd had as a child in the school holidays, exploring the neighbourhood with friends. Time was no issue, because they had all the time in the world. He lay on his back and watched a few silky clouds float around and change shape. He watched the blue of the sky and tried to make out where it deepened into the wonderful place they call outer space. Philip thought of space travel, thought of himself as a man in a rocket headed out from all he knew to discover other life forms and languages.

'Hey,' said James. He was sitting up and pointing down the hill towards the small house on the edge of the section.

Philip sat up. Beyond a wobbly fence and an untidy garden he could see an old man staring out at him and James from a gap in some sheer curtains. The old man was looking directly at both of them. He didn't wave or move much, nothing to signal a greeting; he just fixed them both with a stare.

Philip thought of the baboons at the zoo who had sat watching him and the boys once. They'd been right up the front of their enclosure, so that all the baboons and humans had between them was a pane of thick perspex. Philip and the boys had sat down beside the enclosure and the two groups had watched each other for around twenty minutes. There was a father, and a mother with a baby attached to her front, and another older sibling. At first George and Charlie had laughed and made jokes about their crimson bottoms, but then they stopped talking and moved into a quiet watchfulness that the baboons' own hard gaze demanded of them. Every now and then the mother would pick lice out of her baby's head with her teeth. He's got nits like me, George had said. Staring at Philip and Charlie and George, the baboons had an attitude that suggested they were no more and no less than the animals that had paid to look at them.

Philip nudged James. The old guy was staring out at them still, but he was moving.

'He's stripping,' said James.

It was true: the old man was slowly undressing himself. He unbuttoned his shirt, and they watched him fold it carefully and bob out of view while he placed it on the ground. He had a singlet on underneath and he pulled it up over his head. Then he undid his belt and loosened his trousers.

'Oh,' said Philip. 'Do you think he—?'

He took some time folding his trousers.

The old man's chest was sunken, as if his ribs and lungs had been shrunk. His bony shoulder bones jutted out from beneath his neck and head, his enlarged wrinkled ears. The whole time he folded his trousers, his gaze was steady, straight on them.

Because they were stoned, they didn't stand up and get back on their bikes. Also, Philip told Marilyn later that afternoon when she asked why they had just sat there, it had felt impolite to leave, like walking out halfway through a play in which a friend had a lead role. So they stayed put and watched the old guy as he stripped down to nothing. They saw his thighs, the muscle wasted so that the skin just clung to bone and sinew, and they saw his saggy scrotum—and Philip, fresh from his own brush with mortality, turned away.

'Oh, God,' said James. 'That's us in thirty years.'

The old man was a live performer, a visitor from the future acting out for them their very own fortunes.

But then, Philip told Marilyn later, the old man wiped his arse on the curtains. Marilyn laughed. 'He what?'

When Philip had looked back, the old guy was bent over and was giving the gauze curtains a good going over.

'Oh, he's actually doing that for us,' said James, and he stood up. And then he started to clap, a loud, slow clap.

Philip stood up beside him, because it seemed the thing to do.

The old guy straightened, and scowled at Philip and James as if they were assaulting his privacy. He jerked the curtains closed and lowered his blinds.

'Right,' said James. 'I guess that show's over.' He turned to Philip and smiled. 'God help us.'

They pedalled off slowly down the hill, side by side, not talking but content in each other's familiar company. It didn't take much, thought Philip, to be happy. It didn't take much and yet it did.

In the night Philip woke to rain, hard on the roof. He shivered, a delicious thankful shiver. He put his hand out to touch Marilyn, sound asleep beside him. Rain on the roof was a sort of luxury. They were perfectly warm inside their house, under the covers; the roof did not leak, and they had each other.

He thought of the old man up on the hill—of his pale cadaverous chest and the wasted hanging scrotum. And he was alone. Perhaps his only entertainment was to strip in front of strangers. Philip shook his head slightly on the pillow to try to remove the image of the old man. He forced himself to think only of the rain. To keep his mind there he imagined it was perfectly vertical like rain in a child's drawing. The mind, that great time traveller, rushed back and forth and in and out of shadows on its own course.

And Philip found himself back in Barcelona, with nine-month-old Charlie strapped to him in a baby backpack. Marilyn was at his side. It was late spring and they were excited by the buildings, the imaginative buildings, and the way the people in the streets linked arms and kissed each other when they met.

They were on their way to show baby Charlie off to Philip's sister in London. They'd spent the morning looking at Miró paintings and sculptures. His patterns and dots seemed to Philip like a twentieth-century version of cave paintings, or of the stars in their galaxies, his own imagined inter-planetary wanderings.

They were a few blocks from their apartment when the sky blackened and thunder started to boom above them, the sound echoing around the streets and tall buildings. The first intermittent drops came as dark blooms spreading on their shirts and pants. Marilyn stopped to throw a blanket over Charlie's head.

Then the rain came down. They ran. After half a minute, water was filling the gutters. Their summer sandals splashed in and out of puddles that were forming on the uneven paving. The sky got lit up in blue. Thunder boomed and echoed around the streets. They ran through the roar of the weather, shouting directions and pointing the way back to their apartment, and laughing. They ran and they laughed, and little Charlie, a small person on Philip's back, laughed too.

And when they finally got back to the apartment and stripped off their sodden clothes and took towels to their hair, Philip took a photo of Charlie—of his face shiny with rain, and him beaming at his mother and father like they'd arranged the weather purely for his own entertainment.

Lying in bed just now, Philip remembered this and he thought, These are the moments, just these. The world momentarily lit up in blue and us running through it, wet to the skin.

Acknowledgements

In 'The Bookshop', the line 'somehow a dog/has taken itself & its tail considerably away' is taken from John Berryman's 'Song 14: Life, friends is boring. We must not say so'.

In 'Decay', 'I can change if it helps you fall in love' is taken from the song 'I can change' by LCD Soundsystem.

Thanks to Elizabeth Knox, Sara Knox, Kate Duignan, Pip Adam and Bridget van der Zjipp for their reading of early stories and drafts. Thanks to Hinemoana Baker, Kate Camp, Stefanie Lash, Maria McMillan and Marty Smith for their lively conversation.

Thanks to George and Charlie Symon.

Thanks to Fergus Barrowman for his catholic taste and support. Thanks to Jane Parkin for editorial advice.

Thanks to Gerard Crewdson for making such wonderful pictures to go with the stories.

This book is dedicated to David Long and Marty Smith, the best first readers. My great thanks and love to you both.